A minute later it
trees and thick bus
a shattering grindi
The 'copter veered sideways and Mardie was thrown against Jard. His chin was down and he was working at the controls. An eagle slammed through the windscreen – its beak straight at Jard's head. There were feathers everywhere.

'Put your hands over your forehead, Mardie. Lean forward down against the panel.' Jard seemed to speak in a mumble. '*NOW. Do as you're told.*'

Available in Fontana by the same author

Sweet and Faraway
Come Home Dear
Master of Ransome
The Stranger from the North
Down in the Forest
The Call of the Pines
Follow Your Star
The Man from the Outback
Ranger in the Hills
Reaching for the Stars
The River is Down
Home at Sundown
Six for Heaven
Shining River
Joyday for Jodi
The Bell Branch
The Mountain that Went to the Sea
Ribbons in Her Hair
Pepper Tree Bay

LUCY WALKER

Girl Alone

Collins

FONTANA BOOKS

First published by Wm. Collins 1973
First issued in Fontana Books 1974
Second Impression August 1974

Made and printed in Great Britain by
William Collins Sons & Co Ltd Glasgow

ONE

It was a brown land.

As far as the human eye could see it was this yellow brown.

Flat, except for the occasional clumps of mulga. These were like stick trees since the cyclone's wind had stripped them of leaves. Only in the far, far distance to the east did the land lift in a haze of low mesa-topped hills. The drought and later the cyclone had beggared and bared the land. Except for the stones. They were small, mostly ironstone cobbles, the last remnants of what had once upon a dream-time – milleniums ago – been upland and mountain range. Now – except for this place – The Breakaway – it was gibber country.

Here at The Breakaway, Mardie sat in the store's office and doodled with her pen on a piece of paper. Through the west window she could see the white-trunked gum trees growing along the boundary line. There was a lush garden at the back of the store. Green lawn, flower beds, and citrus trees. On the south side the trellised patio blazed bougain-villaea and oleander. On the north side lay a melon bed. Rock melons, water melons, honeydews.

This flowered tropical glory covering one isolated area in the shield-desert of gibber, mulga and spinifex, was because The Breakaway sat on an underground lake of water. A bore sunk deep and a windmill whirling above the tank-stand did the rest. Water sprayed from sprinklers all over.

After that, and all around, was this desert again. That is except for the distant mesa range. Out there prospectors, explorers, and their camp followers were at work. The great nickel boom was on where once – thirty to fifty years ago – it had all been gold that the prospectors and outbackers had sought and mined.

Mardie stopped doodling and put her pen down. She brushed her hand through her short dark hair, sat back in her chair, and gazed out of the east window at the landing ground on the west side of the road.

'The bitumen' they called this road. It led for nearly two thousand miles from the rich and verdant cities down south by the Swan River, up through the vineyards along the river valley, through the timber-belted Darling Range. Then progress by progress, this bitumen streak of a road ran northwards and onwards through the farm lands, out and up through sheep stations, across the great loneliness of the shield-desert – to the Top End. Maybe right to the Timor Sea for all Mardie knew.

At The Breakaway tracks came in to meet the bitumen. One came from the Never Never north-east, and another from the west. Yet a third, dusty and gravelly, came in from God knew where – south-eastwards. They met, these tracks, touched one another, circled the green heaven of The Breakaway, then joined the north-south bitumen and so on their way.

The real outbackers came to The Breakaway 'stop-over' by these gravel tracks. The through-travellers, perhaps one or two a day – from north or south – used the bitumen.

Mardie had been here one month. Each day she sat at this office table and looked out through one window or another, and wondered at it all. So vast. So lonely. Always the *great silence,* broken only when a light plane, or an occasional helicopter came in on the landing ground on the east side of the bitumen, or maybe when a sheep or cattle truck, a delivery truck, or a car passed up or down along those miles and miles of blue bitumen. Only then did this girl, small, slight, dark-haired and dark-eyed – all alone – hear anything other than this silence. Funny how you can *hear* silence! she thought. The minutiæ of the store's internal clitter-clatter was the sound of an ant world beside it. No more.

The buzzer on the radio fixture buzzed in the room like a muffled alarm. It was the small two-way on a closed circuit, not the main transceiver, now buzzing Mardie. She took the mouth-piece from the hook and spoke.

'Bickleys Brandy,' she said. 'Mardie speaking. Over.'

'Red Wine here, sweetheart.'

A man's voice came into the room as clearly as if its owner were sitting by the door.

'David Ashton, love,' he said. 'The utility from the outcamp left three hours ago and passed through Mansell Downs Station one hour later. You should hear it coming any time now. Be a darling and call the Dig-in when it arrives. Just checking for safety reasons, pet.'

'Message received,' Mardie said. 'Shall keep you informed,

David. Back to you.'

'Be sure to notify Mansell Downs when the ute leaves for the return, Mardie darling.'

'Will do – without fail,' Mardie said. 'And I'm not your darling, David. Not yet, anyway. Tell me about the weather round the Dig-in. It's safer as a subject for conversation.'

'Look out the window, love. It's the same as yours. Blistering hot. Cold at night. And Mardie, my darling, my dear, it's nice to hear your voice. Did you know you have a lovely voice? Over.'

'No, I didn't, and I haven't. Your turn.'

'The men out here are itching to see the Voice's owner. Cross my heart – it's true. Your turn to speak, love. Say something I can dream about.'

Mardie laughed. It was like the fluted sound of angels' wings to the lonely men – all of them – out at the Dig-in Exploration Camp, but Mardie did not know this. She did not believe David. She thought he was a flatterer and only talked this way because he was on a closed circuit, and so was safe. She knew there was a 'female' geologist out there with all those men. Young and pretty too – so Mr and Mrs Richie, the store's managers, had told her. Actually she – this girl – was a geo-physicist – someone who did the analysis and assaying of rock specimens. So they weren't all that girl-hungry, were they? Even if Mardie had known about the 'angels' wings' and her own clear voice, she would not have understood what was meant by the kind of 'male loneliness' that meant each man wanted *his* girl. Not someone shared.

'Thank you for those nice few words,' she said, a laugh in her voice now. ' 'Bye, David. Will call you later when the ute leaves.'

' 'Bye now, sweetheart. Come out and see us some time. We're all agog. Me specially. Out.'

'Over and out,' Mardie said, *almost* sadly.

David Ashton's voice always had something special in it. A kindness, and a bright boyish kind of 'cheek', though its owner had to be older than that. He was *the* chief geologist out there. The man who advised the 'Company' as it were. And reported back to the Exploration Company's headquarters in Sydney. Another two thousand miles away, across two deserts – and what else – to the eastern seaboard.

He was really very nice – Mardie thought just a little wistfully. She understood some kinds of loneliness because she'd been lonely herself – for a long time – before she'd come out here. And that, right in the middle of a city! Always *alone.* Funny how her life had worked out like that!

Funnier still, she thought, how the cat always hears something coming. Seconds before her own ear could detect any sound, the cat had lifted its head. The sound was of a distant gnat of a plane – the one due to bring in Mr Lawson, the solicitor. Too early, Mardie reasoned, for the utility from the Dig-in. She didn't know which she hoped for most.

Then she heard the sound more clearly. It *was* the utility all right – the one coming in from the out-camp, many miles north-east of the Dig-in. Mardie pushed her hair back from her forehead again. The utility had probably come in for the mail as well as the stores, she thought. Who would be driving? That other, *different* geologist again? The mystery man? If hope was a little flame – like lamplight in the dark – she didn't recognize it. So she did not admit it.

The ute swung in from the road, and came to a stop broadside on to the store's track.

Twice before, since Mardie had been here in the north, she had heard that utility stop just that way, in just that place.

She pushed back the chair and thought of going to the mirror, gilt-chained to the office door. What did she look like? If she put on lipstick . . .?

But she wouldn't. *No.* She didn't want to fool even herself.

She hadn't really seen this particular geologist – *close-up.* Only at a distance of quite a number of yards.

He didn't come into the office, ever.

Mr Richie, who managed The Breakaway, generally went out to meet him as if he were some very special person. The geologist usually came into the front entrance, Mr Richie would pack his order, then carry it out to the jeep. Mrs Richie, no matter what she had busily been doing, would come padding in, soft in those foam-soled canvas shoes of hers, and bundle up the mail. Then she'd take it out to the jeep for him. He didn't have to carry his own personal mail, let alone the carton of stores. They just wouldn't let him. Everything was done in a ritual performance, and it seemed that *he* – this important one – didn't want to deprive the Richies of this glad-act of theirs.

Just how important could one man outback be? Mardie wondered about this quite a lot. All she had seen, in the four weeks she had been here, was a tall shadow-man with a brown flop-brimmed cotton hat on his head. And the yellow-brown exploration boots at the ground level. Only this, and no more, as he had passed along the shadow side of the trellis into the service part of the store.

Next she had heard the voices as Mr and Mrs Richie talked to him. Mr Richie's voice was a bit nut-cracking, generally, but always quiet when this particular man came in, Mrs Richie's speech had that thin outback, slow-speaking quality about it. It was hard to hear anyway.

Mardie had early recognized this man's different sort of voice. It was quieter, more deliberate, yet somehow authoritative. None of the other through-travellers and outbackers spoke quite like him.

His name was Jard Hunter. The Richies had told her this when he had come to The Breakaway the first time after her own arrival. They had told her *he* said there was no need to come in and meet her. He was too busy and in a hurry. No time for social contacts.

Yet he hadn't hurried as he'd gone along the shade side of the trellis. He had walked in a casual sort of way. Later he'd gone back towards the utility in the same manner. His hat was each time well down on his forehead so that the upper part of his face was in deep shadow.

Each time he had come, the same routine followed. The yard man carried out two cases of bottled beer to the utility.

'Two cases,' Mr Richie had said, 'because Jard Hunter doesn't allow too much drinking out at his camp. Never too much on the place at a time. A bottle per man a day . . . is his ration.' The big truck, when it came in for the main Dig-in camp – generally a week later – always took out cases and cases of soft drink as well as the heavier loads of stores.

Very indifferent and unfriendly, Mardie thought of Jard Hunter now, as once again she listened to that unmistakable tread as it came down the gravel track, on to the cement path, then along the shade side of the trellis.

Yet there was something about him. Something intangible and unnameable that edged at her curiosity, and at the *aloneness* that was in her too. That funny sort of occasional, yet unpredictable lonely feeling had the better of her again now. Yet she *ought* to get on with the accounts . . .

She pushed back her chair so that she could see through the one window that looked out on to the trellised path.

He walked casually, yet like a man with certainty about him. His head was down, because as he came abreast of the window he kicked away a gravel pebble lying on the cement. She could see his chin, but the rest of his face was shadowed by the flop brim of that brown cotton hat. She heard him go into the bar and then Mr Richie's voice saying something newsworthy to him.

Mardie sighed. Ought *she* to take the initiative and go and make this man's acquaintance? It would be a routine thing to do, wouldn't it? She was the new owner at The Breakaway. It made sense to meet and know the people with whom she did business.

She almost stood up. But didn't.

The Richies had managed the place for years and years and years – like they owned it. She had to leave things that way, for her own sake as well as for the Richies'. She couldn't do without them. Besides, the will – that instrument of part-pleasure, part torture – had laid down that The Breakaway was to remain the Richies' home, so long as they wished to stay there. It had advised the legatee – herself, Marie-Ann Forrester, commonly called Mardie – to retain the Richies as managers and/or advisers so long as they were physically and mentally able.

Thinking of all this, and looking at the cat which had lifted its head again because it had heard yet another distant sound, she remembered what it was she had really been waiting for. It was the arrival of Mr Lawson, the solicitor, who had drawn up the will and who was the trustee. He was coming – really from kindness – to see how she was getting on. He would not be explicit about this because he didn't want his visit to look as if he doubted her wisdom in coming to The Breakaway. He had put all that into plain words three months ago.

'You should simply take over where your godfather left off,' he had advised. 'He went up north to the place once a year to see the Richies, and that was all. He merely *owned* The Breakaway, but didn't run it. The profits have been moderate. But steady. With all this outback pegging for mineral claims – specially nickel claims – he took the precaution of having The Breakaway pegged to safeguard it from prospecting marauders. A firm of professional geologists did that for him. If there was anything worthwhile found, those claims have, in the will, automatically been transferred to you.'

'I wasn't thinking about that,' Mardie had said sadly. 'I was thinking that I loved him. And I didn't let him know. I didn't go to see him very often. I never *told* him I loved him. He was the only one I really had . . .'

'You mean you didn't tell him in as many words. That

happens so often, Mardie. The aftermath for those who loved the person gone is always remorse. In my profession I see it happen every week. Ben Parry would have known you loved him. He would have *known*.'

She had shaken her head. 'No. He had no one else to leave it to, I suppose, being a bachelor. In a way, he too was alone. Like me. Except perhaps for Mr and Mrs Richie.'

'There are other benefits in the will for them. They were very happy and touched that the old man thought of them. A home for life – where they've always been and where there's work to do – is not to be sneezed at, Mardie. The big thing is for you to play it cool, and not to make it hard for them.'

Mardie had looked across the table. 'You are the trustee,' she said quietly. 'You are there to look after their interests too, aren't you?'

Mr Lawson had really smiled. 'You're very discerning, aren't you, my child? Yet you don't look in the least like the "business-head" type.'

'What type do I look like?'

'A gentle, quiet girl – but one with spirit carefully hidden away, I think.'

Mr Lawson had done his best to persuade her not to go outback to live at The Breakaway. 'Go and have a look-see,' was what he had advised. 'Then come back to civilization. I think you *will* come back once you see it's near-desert up there. The west side of a vast shield-desert actually. All but gibber country. You know what that means? Stones. Not soil, not even dried-out earth. Just stones . . . like egg-sized pebbles. There's mulga scattered over it, but that's because the stones are smallish and somehow – when the cyclones bring rain – the mulga, and some grass, grow through them. Of course, The Breakaway is an oasis, alone in that desert.'

All alone too, Mardie had thought.

That was all of three months ago, and now Mardie had been at The Breakaway but a few weeks.

The cat with its lifted head had been right.

Mr Lawson's small Piper plane was wheeling in to land straight into the wind . . . just as the wind bag at the end of the landing ground indicated that it should land. One, two, three bumps and the Piper was down. Slowed. At rest. A gleaming gnat on a base of flat pebble ground.

Mardie had no divided thoughts about looking in the mirror strung to the back of the office door this time. She needed to look her best. She had to convince Mr Lawson all was well with her.

Ever since her father had married again – after her mother's long, long illness – she had felt she had no real home. Her stepmother was good to her. Very kind. Thoughtful too. But Mardie knew she herself was the third person in that household – which meant one too many. Her presence didn't give them a chance. Not *really*. They had to hide their feelings from one another when she was in the same room with them. She was the lone one. They, her father and his new wife, had each other. She had lost all her own social contacts in the long illness of her own mother. Her friends had all gone away, or been married; found new friends and interests.

Now here at The Breakaway, she had a home of her own. It belonged to her, and she belonged to it.

Mardie called the Dig-in and let them know the camp's utility had arrived. Mr Geologist wasn't in his utility now so he wouldn't hear her call. She wanted to ask the sixty-four dollar question.

'Come in, Bickleys Brandy. Over to you.' This was a new voice. A stranger.

'Your utility has arrived . . .' She hesitated, then asked: 'Who was driving it?'

'Same driver, Brandy. Goes by the name of Jard Hunter. Over.'

Mardie sighed. 'I just wondered. Have you always sent the same driver? I'm the new owner here and am just learning the accounts. The account books tell me the stores he picks up go to *his* account. There's a different account for the Dig-in Company.'

'So what? It gets paid, sweetie. Not to worry. We'll let you know each time we collect stores on the Camp's account. Hunter's is a special one. His needs are different on his job. He's a hydro-geologist, exploring for water. Mostly along the mesa range line. So a different camp.'

'I see. I wasn't worrying about payment, you know. I just didn't understand how it worked.' Mardie's voice faded in embarrassment. She couldn't explain curiosity. It wasn't an easy thing to explain. She *did* want to know about Jard Hunter – the man whose face was always shadowed under the brim of that brown hat. Even the Richies were reticent about him. She'd come to call him her 'mystery man' in her mind. Unseen by her listener, Mardie's face was pink with embarrassment. 'We really are on a closed circuit, aren't we?' she asked. 'I mean I didn't want to broadcast business affairs to the world the way one does on the transceiver service. Over.'

She heard a laugh coming through from the other end.

'Closed circuit all right, love. Why don't you come out to the Dig-in some time and we'll show you how it all works. He's after underground water. We're after nickel. We'd like to meet you, Mardie. You talk so nice. Anyone tell you that before?'

'I think you're all flatterers out there at the Dig-in. But thank you. I'd love to come. I haven't seen an Exploration Camp yet. Do you think Jard Hunter might take me some time?'

'Phew! You *are* asking something. He's a loner – that one. He doesn't always come straight here, anyway. He's at his out-camps most of the time. Why don't you ask him yourself? Over.'

'I might do just that. I'll call Mansell Downs on the transceiver and let them know when he leaves. That's a safety rule, isn't it? Over.'

'It's just that . . . in case a kangaroo turns him over, or something. When anyone's travelling distance out here it's practical sense to have a line of communication. 'Bye now, nice voice. We'll call you when to expect the big truck. Over and out, Mardie.'

'Out, Red Wine.' She added 'dear' under her breath. She only knew their voices but they were all so nice to her. A little bit teasing – and full of flattery, of course. But somehow they – voices on the air – made her feel warm inside and wanted. Specially David Ashton. He generally had the latest joke story to tell her. He so often made her laugh – which was a wonderful thing to do – at any time.

TWO

As she had been speaking she had seen Mr Lawson step down from the plane and come walking across the landing ground towards The Breakaway. She longed to get up, go through the door and along the trellised path towards the store part of the building. She could pretend this was in order to announce Mr Lawson's arrival to the Richies. That way, she could come face to face with this Jard Hunter. There would have to be a meeting then, wouldn't there?

But she was too late.

Mr Richie had come out of the store and looked towards the landing ground. He was short, grey-haired, and his face was grooved with lines – all of them cheerful.

He turned and called, 'Mardie! Here comes your VIP. Aren't you going to meet him? Or will . . .'

'I'm coming,' Mardie answered. She put on a hurry-up.

She had to look straight ahead past that beckoning doorway beyond which Mr Mystery Man, hydro-geologist, was doing whatever it was he was doing this moment. She didn't want to show her curiosity.

She ran to the bitumen, then over it as she waved her hand to the approaching man.

Mr Lawson, because of the heat, wore a spotless white shirt and shorts. No coat. His overnight bag and briefcase encumbered him somewhat, so his return wave was half-mast only. But his smile was broad.

'Is a legal adviser allowed to kiss a client?' he asked as Mardie ran up to him. 'A member of the medical fraternity would get the sack if he tried that approach to a client.'

Mardie's glad smile was truly winning. 'I'll do the kissing,' she said happily. 'It won't be your crime then, will it?'

She stood on tip-toe and kissed his cheek, then took his satchel from him.

He slipped his freed arm round her shoulder and gave her a gentle hug. 'My!' he said. 'How sun-tanned you are already. And you look happy. Are you happy, Mardie?'

'Yes. I have something to which I belong. Besides belonging to you too, of course. You are *my* trustee, aren't you, Mr Lawson?'

'Just that technically, Mardie. But I have a belonging feeling towards you too. Do you mind that – from an old codger?' He smoothed down his greying hair which shone in the bright hot sun. His round kindly face beamed pleasure at meeting his young client again.

Mardie hugged his arm. 'Thank you for it being that way,' she said. 'But I know what you're going to ask next. Have I had enough of life at The Breakaway?'

'Well, not next. But some time in the next hour.'

'Well, the answer is . . . *I love it. I'm going to stay,* that is, unless . . .'

He looked at her quizzically. 'Unless?'

'Unless it's too disturbing for the Richies. It's their permanent home and I've already been through that worry of being the *third* person in a household. The sort of extra one. Not needed . . .'

'I'll put your mind at rest on that straight away. Mr Richie in his letter – on *legal matters* – made it happily clear that everything was working out well. They're getting fond of you already, Mardie. He said they're both feeling younger now there's some young life around.'

'That was sweet of him, wasn't it?' Mardie was surprised and touched. She wanted to stay at The Breakaway and build a home and a life for herself. Already she could see how she could make it pay better. For instance, put in some overnight accommodation for weary through-travellers. There was a half acre of space at the side. Put in six or even eight motel-type units . . .

They had reached the road and a great truck, followed by a low-loader piled with steel girders, swept up the length of the bitumen. The whole thing swung angle-wise into the pass track at the side of The Breakaway, then came finally to a grinding halt under the white-trunked gum trees.

'They all stop,' Mardie explained to Mr Lawson, now excited to tell him the wonders of a lone store at the meeting of the ways. '*Everything.* Cars, trucks, freezer-vans, utilities, low-loaders. Even in the middle of the night. Everyone stops. Nothing goes past without someone buying something! Even only a little thing. Sometimes only one or two vehicles pass in a day. Sometimes lots. Some days there's nothing – absolutely nothing goes along the road at all. There's only silence. It's strange – that silence. It's like something that's everywhere. As if the world, all over has stopped. Watching, waiting.'

'Yes, I know. Those who do use the track have to keep The Breakaway here, Mardie. That's against the moment of emergency when they'll *need* it to be here. It's nearer two hundred than one hundred miles to the next stop-over, isn't it? They might need The Breakaway some day in a crisis situation. So they keep it going . . . all of them . . . by stopping. Regardless of real needs.'

'Yes. But it's rather wonderful, isn't it?'

'It's what is called the "unwritten law" of the country, infant. Where there's a safety valve it's in everyone's interest to keep it there. And ticking over too.'

'It's wonderful,' Mardie said again, still awed at the unwritten law that everyone stopped and *bought* something.

Anything. It was a rule that no one broke. The story of the long-distance roads of the outback!

They had reached the cement path under the trellis shadeway now.

A few yards ahead of them a tall figure emerged from the store's doorway. It was Mr Mystery Man Geologist.

He barely turned his head so that all Mardie and Mr Lawson saw was the shadowed brown face, light on a pair of eyes, and the white line of teeth in a bare smile that quickly came and as quickly was gone.

He raised his hand in the familiar outback greeting of man to man in passing, and walked on down the far end of the cement.

He turned the corner of the building. And was gone.

Mr Lawson put his overnight bag down. They stood still for a moment while he looked over the front façade of The Breakaway. He took in the store, the resting place beside it, with the long timber seats against the store wall under the shade of trellised vines, for tired travellers. He glanced to the left at the small house attached to the west side of the main building. This small attached house of timber and iron-roof was Mardie's home and the store's 'Office'.

'He's a strange one . . . *that,*' Mardie said. She looked at the corner around which Jard Hunter had disappeared. Her head was bent as if listening to the fading sounds of heavy outback boots treading casually, yet somehow with intent, over the gravel which led to the utility standing under the shade of a white-trunked gum tree a little ahead of the truck-and-trailer.

Mr Lawson caught the puzzlement in her voice. He looked down at her. 'Who is a "strange one"? You mean the young man who just came out?'

Mardie looked up quickly. '*Young* man?' she demanded. 'He'd be thirty, at least, I mean, I think so. I haven't really seen him. He just comes and goes. Not quite silently, of course, you can always hear that tread. But nearly . . . sort of. Even if there's another truck or car there he doesn't seem to stop to talk. Just lifts his hand, like the way he did just now, and walks on.'

'So that puzzles you? I thought all outback men were like that. Part of the great silence.'

'Oh some – yes! But not all. It's just that he's different. And he's not a through-traveller. He's a geologist, or something. Hydro-geologist they call him. He searches for underground water. Not minerals. There's a big Mining Exploration Company over south-east of that mesa range out there. He comes in from some out-camp for light stores. He wouldn't have lived all his life outback, would he?'

'Could have. Might have been a prospector earlier. Or the son of a grazier or pastoralist. But why the interest?'

He was looking down at Mardie, his eyes inquiring.

Mardie laughed. 'Don't ask me *why*. Just something about the man, I suppose. Almost as if he were a mystery man – which he is not, of course. He's something to do with the Dig-in, I know. That's what they call the exploration camp out there. They always call from the Dig-in on the closed circuit when he's coming in. They sort of watch out for him.'

'From the Dig-in?'

'It's miles and miles away really. Way past Mansell Downs Station. The Dig-in is a hundred miles on from there, I think, though they always talk in "hours" not "miles". I haven't seen it. Mr Richie told me . . .'

Mardie stopped. She realized there was real curiosity in Mr Lawson's interest. There was something alert and watching in his eyes. Perhaps that was only because he was a solicitor!

She caught his arm impulsively. 'He's not all that interesting,' she said, shaking her head. 'Come on in and say "Hallo" to the Richies. They're being tactful and deliberately not coming out so as to let us talk . . .'

'Well, we mustn't keep them waiting any longer. Mrs Richie will be rubbing up the brass again, I'll bet. I know her of old. Expect a house visitor and she'll give the place a spring clean – and cook a dinner fit for kings.'

'Except we don't have spring here. Only summer all the time. Hot, hot summer.'

Mr and Mrs Richie, both grey-haired and cheerful, were waiting behind the tiny bar section of the store. Not for the first time Mardie thought, They really are sweeties. They beamed on Mr Lawson in a near identical manner. They held their hands palm down, waiting, on the edge of the bar. They were both of the same height – she a little stout, and he thick-set and muscle-strong. They had changed into spotless clothes and were holding themselves as if about to receive royalty.

'Good day, Mr and Mrs Richie!' Mr Lawson returned their smiles as he put down his bag and reached across the bar to shake hands with them. 'Nice to see you again. Looking well, as usual.'

'You too, Mr Lawson.' Mr Richie nodded his head as if to add emphasis to this important judgment on his part. 'You're looking fine – as does your wife.'

'You don't even look tired, Mr Lawson,' Mrs Richie said. 'Travelling in those little planes makes most people tired. They bucket about so.'

Mr Lawson glanced round the room. It really was the most remarkable piece of construction. Over the ninety years The Breakaway had been here, there had been alteration added to alteration, piecemeal. All in the most fascinating way. One wall was made of wattle and daub, and the opposite one of old, old timber . . . beautifully maintained. Part of the floor was of old stone, each piece welded to the next by the passing of time and the tread of many heavy, booted feet. Another part – added much later – was made of cement slabs. The coming of motor traffic had made that change. The days of those who had passed through the Breakaway by horseback, horse-cart or even – with the gold finds half a century ago – by camel train, had gone. Each passing phase of The Breakaway's history had left its mark on the place. Strange faded photographs hung in wooden frames, depicting miners, mining rigs; faded newspaper cuttings; somebody's paintings of mulga trees and kangaroos. On a shelf were old bottles, stone flagons of bygone days, a lump of gold-bearing ore, and an Edwardian silver trophy some gold fossiker long gone had won in an outback horse race.

The inside wall dividing the bar from the dining-cum-sitting-room did not reach the ceiling. There was a two-foot gap there. Sitting on this ledge in the space between the two rooms was a row of ornaments. All brass. A bell, a kettle, a tobacco container, a cigarette box and countless smaller, stranger artifacts. The newly-polished brass shone lights into the rich green fern baskets hanging from the ceiling rafter. Two of the main walls were stone and daub. The other two were faced with pressed iron.

Mr Lawson looked around. 'I could come to love this place myself,' he said soberly. 'A museum in its own right. I suppose there are others like it through the old goldfields, but this is the only one I really know.'

'Like the ghost towns!' Mardie said sadly.

'I wouldn't want to live anywhere else,' Jim Richie said firmly. 'But it never was a town here, Mardie. Just a stop-over. Nothing more.'

'His father and his grandfather worked The Breakaway before him,' Mrs Richie announced with an air of pride. 'It was cut off from a corner of the Ben Parry Station property. The station's gone of course. Crown land now. But The Breakaway stayed in the family.'

'You're not likely to live anywhere else, Mrs Richie, unless you wish it,' Mr Lawson said. 'Mr Ben Parry, the last of the family, has seen to that. I have the final papers, yet to be signed with me. Mardie, his godchild, owns the lease of the land from the Crown under my trusteeship while you and your husband live; which is here in your cottage at the north-east side of the store . . . where you've always lived. And you all three have your equal shares in the profits.'

He smiled amiably from Mardie to Mr and Mrs Richie. 'It would be kind of you both to live for ever, Mrs Richie. That way I can have Mardie as my close friend for ever too.' His smile came half circle back to the girl. 'That is,' he added, 'if Mardie can think of a trustee as also a devoted friend.'

'Of course!' Mardie hugged his arm again.

'Well now,' Mr Richie said in his back-to-normal accent. 'It's brandy and dry, isn't it, Mr Lawson?'

'I think we'll all have a drink . . . if we can go into your dining-room, Mrs Richie.'

'On the house!' Mardie and Mr Richie said together.

They all laughed.

Then laughed again because they'd all four laughed *together.*

They were still exchanging stories of the old days over their drinks in the adjoining room when the sound of a motor vehicle coming full belt from the north down the bitumen broke the outside silence.

Jim Richie cocked his head, listening. 'That's Hunter's ute coming back,' he said, pushing back his chair. 'Not like him to forget anything. Never knew him muff a thing. A terror for thoroughness is Jard Hunter.'

Mardie lifted her head, listening. Then she caught Mr Lawson's eyes watching her.

'Well . . . you never can tell,' she said lamely, caught out with that sudden jerk of the head. 'Mr Richie can't always be right. I mean one utility sounds like another, doesn't it? It could be our next customer passing through.'

'Not to my husband,' Mrs Richie said emphatically. 'He can almost pick one cockatoo from another when those flocks come overhead. Very acute hearing, Mr Richie has.'

'In that case,' Mr Lawson said easily, 'we'd better accept the fact that Mr Hunter is not infallible, and for once has forgotten something.'

Jim Richie had gone to the door.

The utility had swung into the gravel pass on the far side of the building and spluttered, scattering stones, to a stop. A car door slammed. A heavy tread crossed the gravel towards the cement path under the trellis way.

'Hunter all right!' Jim Richie said again. 'Excuse me, Mr Lawson, I'll just go see what he wants.'

Mardie had all but to pin herself to her chair. After all, *he* . . . whoever it was anyway . . . was *her* customer too. She had a vested interest in customers. Why shouldn't she go and do business with this one, as with others?

Yet she stayed where she was, quite still, except that she moved her glass one inch forward on the table with one small sun-browned hand, while she brushed invisible crumbs from her lap with the other. Funny, she thought, if it were anyone else I'd just go out automatically. Why not this one? Why all the mystery? Is it because, being a geologist, he's more interesting than station owners or drill riggers?

She did not lift her eyes for fear Mr Lawson would be looking at her again. That particular quizzical expression he'd been wearing on his face disturbed her.

Two men's voices could be heard outside. Jim Richie's muted nutcracker followed by a quieter, steady voice with faint undertones of determination about it.

That hint of drawl again! Mardie thought. Funny how men who live in the outback come to speak slowly. Yet they can put the flick of a whip in it when they like. He must be a real outbacker, after all.

Mr Lawson was watching the door. Mardie was sure there was something knowledgeable in the expression in his eyes.

'Will you excuse me, please?' Mrs Richie said, getting up – very agilely, considering her weight and age. 'Jard might like some lunch now. He wouldn't wait before.'

'Of course.' Mr Lawson was also standing. 'What about you, Mardie? Have you something important to do which I mustn't interrupt? It is mid-day.'

'No, nothing.' She was surprised. 'You're my most important occasion.' She laughed, and this lit up her face. Her eyes and even her hair seemed to take on an extra sheen.

Mr Lawson reached in his pocket for his cigarettes.

'I have a feeling you might prefer other company . . . that is, at this moment.' He was looking at her quizzically again.

Mardie beetled . . . just that little bit.

'Ever since you came in, we've been haunted by that beastly man, Jard Hunter. That is, because I said he was a "strange one" when he was going off earlier. You've been looking at me at every mention of his name, haven't you? As if I have some kind of *interest*–' She broke off. 'It's only that he's a puzzle,' she finished lamely. 'I've never even *seen* him properly. Let alone spoken to him.'

Mr Lawson lit his cigarette. He looked over the still flaring match at the girl. Mardie was now standing.

'Haven't you?' he asked amiably. 'I mean, an interest in him? Most people do, I understand.'

'Well . . .' she protested. '*Everyone* here is interesting. Even a funny old prospector who walks miles and miles in here with string hanging round the brim of his weather-beaten hat to keep off the bush flies is interesting. He's so brown he's nearly black. And he's old and can hardly speak because he's forgotten how . . . I mean, living out there alone.'

Mr Lawson's smile became a grin, and the match's flame burned his fingers. He flicked it out and said, 'Damn.'

He came round the table and slipped his arm along Mardie's shoulder just as he had done when they had crossed the landing ground. 'Shall I let you into a confidence? I'm interested in the man myself . . .'

He broke off because Mr Richie had appeared in the doorway. At his side, just a little behind him, was that tallish, wiry-slim man in the act of removing his cotton hat.

Mardie couldn't see the colour of his eyes because, after the bright sunlight outside, he had to half-close them in an effort to identify Mr Lawson. He was burned brown, yet a living kind of brown because of his eyes. They were keen, steel-like eyes, though shuttered as if accustomed to give nothing of himself away. They were aloof, somewhat superior, yet oddly enough kind, as if they *saw* first and judged later. It was no fault of theirs if they saw too much.

His hair was a dark brown too, and his boots were the dusty, rusty yellow geologists' boots that mining explorers wore. He was slim, but a very strong man altogether. And very impressive. Mardie didn't know why he was this last, because he was so quiet. And sort-of very still.

He wasn't looking at her now, but at Mr Lawson. It seemed

as if he knew him.

'Your plane pilot,' Mr Richie explained to Mr Lawson, 'has been talking to Jard Hunter here. You know . . . their air-to-ground radio contacts. The pilot mentioned he'd dropped you here at The Breakaway, Mr Lawson. Jard's come back because he wants to see you, you being a solicitor, I expect.'

'Yes, I am that,' Mr Lawson said. He held out his hand as Jard Hunter took a step forward. The two men shook hands. To Mardie it seemed as if they looked at one another straight in the eyes. Yet they did not exactly smile. It was almost as if they knew one another, yet did not say so, which was strange.

'I wonder if you have a few minutes to spare, Mr Lawson,' Jard Hunter said.

'Of course. In the meantime you must meet Mardie Forrester.' He paused, then added: 'You haven't met before, I understand?'

'No, I think not.' Jard Hunter turned and shook hands with Mardie. He looked right at her, almost in a discerning way as if he were seeing everything about her. Then *knowing* about her – which was disconcerting.

She saw that his eyes were not steel, after all. They were a bluey-grey.

'I had heard that you were here, Miss Forrester,' he said. Her hand was still in his.

He doesn't want to smile, Mardie thought. Not even out of politeness. Then for one split second he contradicted that thought. He did smile. It was an errant smile, quickly come and quickly gone. Yet it had something in it that flashed, like light on a shadowed pool.

Just for one moment Mardie had a strange feeling of regret, as of something found, then lost. Which was ridiculous because it was inexplicable.

She *knew* Mr Lawson had seen the flush she felt rising – just that much.

Suddenly she did the last thing she really wanted to do. She exempted herself from 'the presence'.

'I'm so sorry,' she said. 'I have something that needs my attention. It's important. You will excuse me, won't you?'

She walked through the door, hoping it was with the dignity of a responsible person carrying some of the world's problems on her youngish shoulders. And not just a scatter! The so-called problems were the intricacies of The Breakaway's accounts system, of course.

Back in her office, Mardie examined herself in the mirror hanging by its gilt chain on the back of the door.

What did she really look like? She didn't know. She saw a girl with dark hair, dark eyes and faintly flushed cheeks. She wished she could see something that would tell her she was beautiful, but she knew this would not be true. She was unable to read the kindness and gentleness that was in her face because she did not understand they were there. She was twenty-one, which seemed an archaic age to her. Most of the friends she once had had were married long since. In their teens.

She felt very alone again – with that face in the mirror looking at her so seriously – and very unsure.

Actually she had beautiful, warm-coloured eyes, but she didn't recognize this. Her mouth was well shaped, and when she smiled it, too, was beautiful. But just now she wasn't smiling. Had she been, she would have seen white, even teeth that shone. She took care of them.

Her hair now . . .

Her thoughts kept sneaking back to Jard Hunter. Well, his hair was neat too, because outback even the very modern men couldn't wear it longish. All that heat! But he did have a mention of side-burns. It was his eyes she had noticed most. Not exactly cold, but somehow communicating. He must have been thinking *something*.

Mardie went back to her table and sat down. You have to be thinking something, she repeated to herself. You can't stop thinking. I've tried. Something goes on in your head all the time. Well, what went on in Jard Hunter's head when he met a person for the first time? Especially someone new who had come to live in the area.

Perhaps he wouldn't care a hoot, in which case he wouldn't be thinking after all. Well, nothing in particular anyway!

She pulled the Day Book towards her impatiently.

What the heck, anyway? she asked herself. If anything, it would be about nickel sulphides and gossans, and costeans and claim-pegging, and other such things that fill the minds of geologists. In fact, geologists probably never thought of anything else much . . . except . . .

Why had he wanted to see a *solicitor*?

Mardie flicked over the page of the Day Book and wrote the date at the top of the new page.

Maybe he's going to climb a mesa mountain out there, or slip-slide down one of the gorges. Therefore wants to make a will, she thought. Geologists did sometimes get lost, and one had been killed in an accident some few months ago. She supposed it was a sensible thing to make a will, specially if there was a wife, and children, to think about.

Did he have a wife and children?

THREE

Mr Richie's footsteps came in his odd-beat manner of walking, down the covered trellis way, then through the door.

'You didn't finish your lunch, Mardie,' he began. 'I've brought you some tea – just to fill the gaps, you know. Save you boiling up that jug of yours.'

Mardie smiled. Though she didn't know it, her smile came easily and lit up her face, like a rainbow lights up a sky.

'Why didn't you bring two cups, Mr Richie?' she asked. 'Then we could have had a little talk. That is, while Mr Lawson is so busy with Mr Hunter. Where is Mrs Richie?'

'What's wrong with our having a talk without my having to drink tea along with it?' Mr Richie demanded as he set the small tray on the table. 'I had mine in the kitchen the way I always do. My wife . . . she likes to get on with her work.'

'I hope she gave our visitor . . . I mean *both* visitors, some tea too? Or maybe coffee? I should have gone outside to help her. I sort-of was absent-minded.'

Mr Richie was already at home in the old cane chair beside Mardie's table. He hadn't admitted it yet, but he enjoyed sitting talking to this young girl. Something new and fresh and vital had come into The Breakaway with Mardie's arrival. He and his wife had been very perturbed at first. What were they going to do with a young girl fresh out of a city? Then here had come Mardie! She might be twenty-one and capable, but she was younger-looking than that, and wore bright, fresh-looking clothes. They covered up her knees real decent, thank God. Just right for the outback. Good leather on her feet for working in the garden, too.

Mr Richie had not known that boots were all the fashion in the city now so he took Mardie's ankle lace-ups as a sign of good sense. What's more, she was a real goer in that garden. She really loved it. Well, who wouldn't . . . out here in the middle of a desert?

'Well, about that tea – oh yes! They had a tray with everything on all right, Mardie. The big three-quarter pint cup for Jard Hunter like he always gets when he has time enough to spare, which isn't often. My wife keeps it specially for him. She always calls it "Jard's cup". And let anyone else reach for it by accident!'

'Why is he so special, Mr Richie? He's just a customer like everyone else, isn't he?'

'Oh, no. Not on your life, Mardie. There's customers and customers. All welcome and most of them decent enough. Haven't struck a *real* baddie in years, though there's a few of them about "claim-jumping" since they made that big nickel strike at Kambalda and started the nickel boom. There's a real money-making racket in spying for information about who's finding nickel, where, and how much, all right. They sell the information to townies, and up goes the share market! But Jard's kind of a special because he's a real nice fella when you get to know him. Good manners. Always speaks nicely to my wife. She'd do anything for him.'

Mardie looked down at her cup as she put it back on the saucer.

'What exactly does he do?' She looked up, hoping to seem and sound casual. Not at all that *really* interested. 'We do carry a separate account for him, don't we? The Dig-in is not his real address, is it? His out-camp is somewhere miles out beyond . . .'

Mr Richie laughed. 'Don't you worry about his account, Mardie. He's as straight as they come. Mind you . . . you've a right, being new here, to get acquainted with all the accounts. Specially those that carry them personally and not in a company name. You see, he's a consultant for the company. On his own, that is. Not employed like those others at the Dig-in. Doing a job on contract, as it were.'

'I wasn't really questioning his account,' Mardie put in quickly. 'I suppose . . . well, it was just curiosity as to how these Mining Exploration Companies run their affairs. He seemed to be of importance to the Dig-in Company. Yet he doesn't exactly belong. Being a consultant means he operates on his own, I suppose. He appears out of nowhere – except for the Dig-in's radio call on the closed circuit.'

'Well, that's the way he works.'

'Then he disappears out into nowhere again – without even wanting to get acquainted with a newcomer in the store,'

Mardie said, still puzzled. 'I mean, all the regular through-travellers have come in and shaken hands with me. If it hadn't been for Mr Lawson arriving, I don't suppose I'd ever have met him face to face.'

'Well, he's what they call a "loner", Mardie. He has a special job to do with water, and that has an important connection with the Dig-in. I couldn't tell you how it all works out myself. One doesn't ask questions about what they're exploring. How, when or why. Elsewise they might think we're feeding out news to those spying.'

'Spying?' Mardie exclaimed. 'But why? At the Dig-in they're only looking for nickel or silver, or something, aren't they?'

'Yes. But supposing they find something good? They have to let their Company in Sydney know first. And their "find" has to be tested, or whatever they call it, before it's made public. If somebody lets the cat out of the bag too soon about their "find", if any, then up goes the stock market sky-high. When the stuff is tested, and if it doesn't turn out so good, then down goes the stock market with a thud. You could probably hear it across the Gibson Desert. If it's good, the Company wants to get rich first, doesn't it? I guess that's how it works. We don't ask questions. That way our customers trust us. The less we know the better. Everyone trusts us here at The Breakaway.'

'I suppose so,' Mardie said thoughtfully. She was still puzzled.

'It's a fact of life, young miss,' Mr Richie said cheerfully. 'Out there at the Dig-in, they have rifles to warn off intruders. And a plane and a 'copter of their own to go up and track down any strangers lurking about in the bush. Mr Lawson came in someone's Company plane. Not the usual one. Maybe Jard has something to do with *that*, for all we know, or ask. That wasn't the usual Company's plane brought him down on the landing ground. I saw that for myself.'

'Wasn't it?' Mardie said. She was trying to piece things together. Puzzle one – the plane that brought Mr Lawson wasn't the ordinary service plane then. Its pilot had spoken on an air-to-ground circuit to Jard Hunter, which meant he was on the same wave-length as the Bickley's Brandy-Red Wine code. Puzzle two – Jard Hunter's location was at some distant out-camp, yet the Dig-in knew where he was all the time. Kangaroos on the road, or an accident, they'd said.

Add the fact Jard Hunter himself was like a wraith that

came . . . well, not in the night . . . but came. And went *in silence.* He didn't meet people. Or talk to them unless he had to. Was he a 'watcher in the bush' too? For the Dig-in Exploration Company – or for some other Company watching what Dig-in did? Meantime the people out at the Dig-in were watching him!

Well, so it all seemed!

Puzzle, puzzle! Yet she didn't like to put such strange ideas to Mr Richie. The Richies had always been simple outback people. Storekeepers. Couldn't someone clever enough put anything over them?

Oh dear! *Why* was she thinking such fearful things? It was just Jard Hunter's mysterious manner. Someone ought to tell him to do something about it.

Or was she just sore because he hadn't willingly come in to meet her? Wounded vanity?

The cup only had dregs of tea in it now, but Mardie lifted it to her lips to drain the last drop. Somehow the act was meant to hide her straying thoughts. He was so impressive and strong-minded – that man. Yet his reserve and those shielded yet searching eyes held something unidentifiable about them.

Mardie put down the cup again. She shook her head, as she caught Mr Richie's eyes. She smiled ruefully.

'Somebody told me before I came up here that I'd either hate the outback or that the outback would get me in. If it did get me in I'd better stay here for keeps because I'd never be truly rational again,' she said with a laugh. 'I think the strangest things already. Too much imagination, I guess.'

'Then stay here for keeps. What's important about being rational if you like the place? Good-on the country if it gets you in. And what's wrong with imagination? It's an asset. There's people out way back never seen a town in their lives. Don't even want to . . .'

'Oh, it has me in all right. And I'm not going to worry about being rational or not – *yet*.' Her laugh was the sound of angels' wings again, but there was only Mr Richie – not David Ashton – to hear it. And be grateful for it.

Mr Lawson had come and gone. All the final papers had been signed, and Mardie was now in fact – all the way to the last comma and dot – the owner of The Breakaway. Mr and Mrs Richie had a home for life. In addition, the three of them – James and Mabel Richie and Mardie Forrester – held a three-part partnership in the store's business and all its profits.

Mr Lawson had come – apart from his legal duties – to reassure himself that Mardie not only *meant* what she said about making her home here in the Never, but was happy and determined to make it work out financially. The expression on Mardie's face, her ready smile, the look of good health about her, had put his mind at rest. Even the Richies seemed to have taken a new lease of life now there was a younger person to join their way of life.

Well, they do have someone to take care of them in their old age . . . when it comes, he had thought, mulling over the situation. On the other hand, some up-and-coming young fellow will brush in here one day and clap a wedding ring on Mardie's finger. What then? She's too pretty – kind and gentle, yet basically strong-minded, to be passed over by every jackeroo round the station country. Someone's bound to sweep her off her feet one day.

His thoughts broke off because when that word *someone* came into his mind, a picture of Mardie's eyes following Jard Hunter as he had left The Breakaway the previous day had sprung up in place of thoughts. He shook his head.

Well, that would be a lost cause, he reflected. Jard Hunter is out of bounds for anyone unless it's that possessive young woman geologist they have out at the Dig-in. She has brains and looks and an occasional predatory look in her eye. Joanna Seddon, they tell me, is her name. I must check up on her some day.

He had packed his briefcase with that last thought on the matter.

Mr Lawson was, amongst other legal activities, the solicitor for the Dig-in Company. This was a professional matter which he had kept to himself while at The Breakaway. Clients' affairs were strictly confidential. He had been once only out to the camp but the head geologist, David Ashton, had seen him along with the Company's manager from time to time in his city office. Next time they had a Company meeting he would mention that he would like to meet Joanna Seddon. There was more than one woman geologist working out in the field round Australia he knew, but it would be interesting to meet one of them, specially someone near Mardie's age. He felt she should have someone of her own generation to provide 'young' companionship.

'Mr Lawson seems to know Jard Hunter all right,' Mr Richie said later. 'They shook hands the way people do when they know one another. But he didn't say a word. Solicitors are very close people, aren't they? I guess they have to be, looking after other people's affairs the way they do.'

'Jard Hunter went away again without saying goodbye,' Mardie said, her chin up that little bit which showed she was in her strong-minded stance for the moment. 'I think I shall decide *not* to like him. Everyone in the outback is friendly. They always stop at The Breakaway. It's the law of the country to be friendly. Even if they only pretend – '

'Well, I'm sorry, Mardie, but I guess you not liking him is not going to affect Jard Hunter one bit. He's a "loner". He has to be in a job like the one he has. That is, he's a "loner" except for that girl out at the Dig-in. But then she's professional, like he is. Same sort of job. Only he's a different kind of geologist, they say. Some speciality or other. I forget the word. It's so darn long. But it has something to do with water – not nickel or copper or gold . . .'

'Hydro-geologist,' Mardie said promptly. 'I saw something in the paper about hydro-geologists when the mining boom first started. The article said you can't have mines without water. The geologists explore for rocks, then, if they find something important, they bring in the hydro-geologists to find water – if any. They have a drilling rig just like the ones the geologists use for minerals or oil.'

'That's about it. I know when Jard Hunter came up this way first he was darn interested in The Breakaway because it sits on an underground lake, or something. Said he'd come back some time and map its extent. How deep under the ground – or wide – or something . . .'

'Everyone's interested in The Breakaway,' Mardie said proudly. 'As soon as they come over that rise along the bitumen and see the windmill and trees, then the garden, they say, "*Good heavens! Out here! I don't believe it!*" '

'Jard Hunter believed it all right. He told me he knew about the big artesian wells under part of our outback when he did his studies to be a geologist.'

'Hydro-geologist,' Mardie corrected. 'And not a very civil one, either. Do you suppose they taught him good manners when they taught him to be . . . well, whatever he really is?'

'You've just said what he really is. A hydro-geologist.'

'Yes, I suppose so. What a long word to have to remember.' Mardie was thoughtful all over again. 'I was thinking of something else he might be . . .'

She caught Mr Richie's inquiring eye and laughed. 'Just my imagination,' she said. 'It sometimes runs riot.'

'You mean that girl, Miss Seddon, out at the Exploration Camp? Well, I'd be a bit guarded about attaching too much importance to that. These affairs come and go. But one never can tell. Every man, even a quiet one like Jard Hunter, has 'em, I guess. She's one with a will of her own, I can tell you!'

Mardie's chin lowered itself. A rather bleak look came into her eyes.

One's will acts in funny ways, she thought. It sort-of operates without one thinking about it first.

Mardie didn't have to wait long to meet Joanna Seddon.

Several days later the big truck came in from the Dig-in. This time it was to load up a fortnight's stores for the main camp.

High in the driver's cabin, snug in the passenger's seat, sat a handsome young woman.

Joanna Seddon wasn't dusty, nor was she rigged out in tough workman-like khaki drills. She was downright pretty and wore the brightest cotton dress this side of the Gibson Desert.

'Hallo!' Joanna called gaily as she opened the cabin door. 'You don't mind my calling you Mardie, do you? I've heard them talking to you over the two-way from the Dig-in.'

'Of course not.' Mardie smiled a welcome as she hurried across the gravel driveway. 'We were expecting the truck in from the Dig-in, so you *have* to be Joanna Seddon.'

'None other.' Joanna slipped down from the drop from the cabin as easily as a trained athlete. 'Only one woman out there so if the truck's coming in, plus a female, that's me.'

She stood, taking Mardie in. She twirled a khaki cotton hat, almost identical with the one Jard Hunter wore, round and round her forefinger.

The hat doesn't go with the dress, Mardie thought, then regretted that same thought. It wasn't all that kind, but on the other hand Joanna was taking *her* in, and who knew whether the other girl's thoughts were kind or otherwise? Her sun-tanned, attractive face was smiling in a way that Mardie felt rather than thought was more a smiling manner than something real from right inside her. But then they were strangers. They were two girls nicely somewhere under twenty-five – the only ones in that age group for hundreds of miles around – so they ought to be all but falling on one another's shoulders. Yet there was a reticence. A funny sort of momentary silence.

'Come on in!' Mardie said quickly. 'The sun is killing me, if not you. You won't mind if I treat you as a visitor rather than a customer? It's quite a while since I've seen someone my own age, except for some of the roustabouts going through with the shearing teams.'

'And a quaint lot they are,' Joanna said. 'Of course, I never – but *never* – treat myself as a customer unless I'm looking at a five-thousand-dollar emerald – or some such. Thank you, I was just thinking of coming in myself.'

'An emerald?' Mardie asked, puzzled. They walked across the drive-in towards Mardie's door. 'I thought emeralds were only for the rich. We don't stock any here at The Breakaway, I can promise you.'

Joanna laughed in a slightly condescending way. Mardie felt temporarily very inferior about such matters as to who was rich and who was not.

'There is a mining boom on, you know,' Joanna said. 'Even the roustabouts get rich overnight provided they pick the right stock.'

'And geologists too? I suppose they have what's called "inside information"?'

'Well, they find the stuff, you know. Nickel, copper, silver or whatever. Now, there's this prospector at Cue who has found the second largest emerald in the world! I never see even a hint of sulphides that I don't want to get down on my knees and kiss it – let alone emeralds. That's before we even find out the amount of mineralization – if any.'

'But how do the roustabouts know so quickly?'

They had reached the door and Mardie held the wire screen open for her guest to enter.

'Roustabouts? Oh dear!' Joanna laughed. 'Well, even if they're only baling-up the wool on the stations they still have two days a week – Saturday and Sunday – to snoop around. And snoop around is what they do.' She flopped in the easy chair before Mardie had time to offer it. She examined the fingernails of her left hand. 'Then there's always the grapevine,' she added. 'We start drilling through the gossan at seven in the morning and by seven at night the two-ways to the stockbrokers in the city burn up the air. Sometimes spy planes come overhead, flashing true or false news like moon rays all over.'

She looked up and gave Mardie a summing-up look. 'You ought to get in on it like everyone else out here, Mardie. You might get rich, or you might get your fingers burned. But it's good for the adrenalin while it lasts. Peps you up no end – just to be in on it.'

That word 'spy-plane' had touched a prickly patch somewhere in Mardie.

'Will you have a drink first, and tea later on?' she asked. 'Or . . .'

'Just tea, thank you. I'd love some. Your water here is a long way better than ours out at the Dig-in. We've a bore – slightly saline. A limited amount of better stuff in plastic balloon tanks we import.'

Through the wire door Mr Richie could be seen taking the truck driver towards the store then probably through to the bar. It was a thirsty country and the store did a good business in any kind of cold drink – be what it may.

Mardie had gone to a side table where she kept a hot water jug, a jar of instant tea, and a biscuit tin.

'Mr Richie told me Mr Hunter was very interested in our water here,' she said. 'He's a hydro-geologist, I understand?' Her back was turned and her hands were busy with the tea things.

'So you've met our Jard, have you?' Joanna's voice was very non-committal. Too much so. 'I've always understood he's not given to chatting by the wayside.'

'He's been in once or twice but I didn't meet him till his last call. He came back to meet a visitor we had from the south.'

'*Who?*'

Mardie turned round, surprised at the note in the other girl's voice. Joanna was sitting in a sprawled yet somehow not ungraceful way in the chair. Her khaki-coloured cotton hat was twirling round on her forefinger again. Her head was fractionally lowered, but her eyes were bright and pinpointing like a laser beam directed straight across the room into Mardie's eyes.

FOUR

There was a chilled silence.

'Well,' Mardie said at length, hesitating. 'He was a personal friend of mine. I think they must have met before. I think he . . . well . . . just wanted to see him. I mean Mr Hunter just wanted . . .'

'Call him Jard and be done with it, Mardie. Even the scrawniest prospectors who've never seen a town's lights call him just that and nothing more. The "Mister Hunter" bit makes you sound a "townie" out here in the outback. Even the established station owners and their wives view the "townies" with disdain.'

'Sorry. Mrs Richie warned me about that. When in the outback, look like it. And sound like it too, it seems.'

'Wiser not to forget the customs of the country. It's almost the same thing as legal if you want to get on with people.'

The water had reached boiling point and Mardie brought the jug to the table. Why, she wondered, had Joanna switched from questions about Jard Hunter and his meeting with Mr Lawson to giving advice about the customs of the country?

'Milk?' she asked. 'Or do you like to pour your own?'

'No milk, thank you. One learns to drink tea hot, black and strong, along with all the men out at the Dig-in. I've discovered it's more thirst-quenching that way, too.'

The hint of tension in the air seemed to have evaporated. They were two girls back to being sociable. Friendly too, Mardie hoped, but she was still a little intimidated by Joanna's air of authority.

'I guess I'm scared of scientists,' she said with a laugh as she passed the cup of tea, then the tin of biscuits, across the table to Joanna. 'I'm afraid my expertise goes only as far as typing and a limited knowledge of book-keeping. What shall we talk about? It can't possibly be the weather because it's always the same . . .'

'Yes, I know. Blistering hot. Drops forty degrees at night inland. But you get used to it, and I like it.'

'You like working out there with an Exploration Company?'

'Of course. Otherwise I wouldn't be doing it. The few women geologists who have been produced by the universities have usually been condemned to an office job interpreting maps or recording assays and mining reports. Me? I'm all for Women's Lib, you know.'

'Me too. Well, only in a limited way. Some of it. But not all,' said Mardie, sipping her tea. 'Specially about washing up three times a day, and scrubbing floors. All the same, I'd like to get married some day, which means I must like men. And I need my bras for sheer comfort's sake so I'm not likely to burn them.'

'Me too,' Joanna said, sipping her tea. 'About marrying, I mean. At least one man. I put up scare-off signs all round when I set my hat on any one in particular.'

Joanna's words made Mardie think of Jard Hunter. She had no idea why. Maybe it was that curious look that had the killer instinct about it when Joanna had asked who Jard Hunter had come back to see at The Breakaway. Had it been something to do with grapevines and spy-planes? Or the possibility of another girl? Heavens! Her imagination must be running riot again. If so – *why*?

'How do you get on with all those men at the Dig-in?' Mardie asked. 'One woman and thirty men! However do you manage them?'

'Easily. *I* do the managing. You see, they all like my cooking.'

Mardie threw back her head and laughed. 'A scientist and a good cook all in one,' she said. 'I dips my lid, Joanna.'

'Well you might. But it's *my* way of life and I like it. Talking about clothes, where did you get that extra nice frock? Not put on for someone special who might drop in, by any chance?'

Mardie missed the point of that question because her own reaction to it was to think of Mr Lawson.

'I was busy admiring *your* dress,' she said innocently. 'It's a charmer.'

Joanna sipped more hot tea.

'Oh, that was to impress the truck driver,' she said over the rim of the cup. 'He's like your Mr Richie. He likes a woman to look womanly when driving with him.' She imitated the driver's voice: '"Can't stand women all got up like they're men. *Trousers*! 'S all wrong . . ."'

Mardie laughed. 'Mr Richie doesn't put it that way. He says – at regular intervals: "Isn't it nice to see a young girl in a pretty dress, Mum? Good thing *you* never took to wearing those trousers or those shorts!"'

'He's not with it,' Joanna said briefly. 'It's hot pants now. Anyway, imagine Mrs Richie's figure in shorts – let alone hot pants.'

'For heaven's sake, you don't wear them out at the Dig-in, do you?'

'I would if I wanted to but the sunshine's all wrong. I'd have the skin blistered off me in five minutes. No. I wear shorts and shirt when I'm working. The same khaki drill as the men wear. Slacks when the day's job is over.'

'And the real working hat!' Mardie added, looking at the brown cotton flopper now in pride of place at the end of the table.

'Oh well . . .' Joanna was nonchalant again. 'We all wear them. The pastoralists wear the broad-brimmed sundowners. It's a sort of trade mark. The customs of the country again.'

'And the mining men wear the khaki floppers!' Mardie started to laugh. 'It's funny, isn't it? It's the women who're supposed to be fussy about wearing the right thing. Yet it's the men who go into professional "uniform" – if we can call it that. A mining man, I suppose, would drop dead before he wore a pastoralist's hat, and vice versa.'

'How right you are! That was good tea, Mardie. May I have another cup? And while you're pouring it, how about answering my question? Who did Jard Hunter come to The Breakaway to see?'

The mood had suddenly changed. There was that note of command again in Joanna's voice.

Mardie had her back turned while she set the hot water jug to boil again. She was trying to think quickly. Was there any reason why she *shouldn't* tell Joanna that Jard Hunter had come back to see Mr Lawson? Probably because Mr Lawson was a solicitor? Why was there any mystery in the situation? All that talk about spy-planes and, later, about Mr Lawson being a legal man. What had the spies – with or without planes – to do with Jard Hunter anyway . . . except what she was dreaming up herself? Oh, if he only came and went the normal way instead of like a wraith! Then vanishing to talk on a closed circuit to a plane's pilot way up in the sky. The plane that had brought Mr Lawson in had not been the usual service plane either! Whatever went on was not *her* business. Was it Joanna's?

'Have you gone into a day-dream, Mardie?' Joanna asked again in that controlled yet commanding voice.

'Oh . . . I'm sorry. I was watching the water come to the

boil again. I do hate tea made from water that's not boiling. Yet if the water boils over some of it might get into the connection and we'd have a "short".'

'You're actually *scared* you might get an electric shock? I don't believe it!'

Mardie decided on the instant *not to be put down* like a little girl any more. She looked over her shoulder.

'Yes,' she said flatly. 'How's that for honesty?'

Joanna laughed. 'Good for you!' she said. 'Just for your future piece of mind any shock you received from *that* line would do you more good than harm. It would snap you out of day-dreaming, and improve the elasticity of your mind. That's all!'

Mardie never did answer that question of Joanna's about Jard Hunter. Mrs Richie had come in to ask if the visitor would like a meal.

'No, thank you,' Joanna said, just that small bit bluntly. 'I've had tea and biscuits and that's about my ration figure-wise. Would you please tell Ben . . . that's my truckie . . . not to waste too much time eating – or drinking.' She paused as she brushed crumbs from her frock, then went on: 'He has to load up and he's the one who has to manipulate the truck over that river crossing. It's been on the side-dip ever since we had last season's cyclone.'

Mardie noticed Mrs Richie's back stiffen but she answered politely. After all, Mrs Richie would be reasoning that Miss Seddon was a customer and even out here in the Never the 'customer was always right.'

'I don't like to give orders to your man, Miss Seddon,' she said. 'He is your man. But I will do so if you say so.'

'I do say so,' Joanna said. Her eyes were taking in Mrs Richie as if she were taking in all the aspects of the latest specimen from the depths of the Dig-in's bore.

Mardie didn't want to dislike Joanna but she very nearly did so then.

'*I'll* tell him, Mrs Richie,' she offered cheerfully. 'After all, I've met all the other truckies who pass through. I'd like to meet the one from the Dig-in.'

She moved towards the door with a light step. Joanna's eyes did not miss Mardie's readiness.

'Don't ask him any questions,' she cautioned. 'That is, other than about his health, or the state of the tracks.'

Mardie stopped in her tracks. She turned and looked at Joanna. 'I beg your pardon?' she said.

Joanna had not moved from her original posture in the chair. The tea-drinking was finished, and the brown cotton hat was twirling again on the forefinger.

'The *grapevine*. Remember? Truckies are regarded by some people as the favourite source of information as to what is going on, where and how, in any mining exploration.'

'You think I would ask that sort of question?' Mardie said quietly. 'I'm sorry, but you're quite mistaken. I'm interested in The Breakaway as a stop-over and I hope to build some accommodation quarters for overnighters. That is the limit of my interests in the area, at the moment.'

Joanna laughed. 'Well, don't be hoity-toity, Mardie. Remember you're the new girl up here and the mining exploration world is foreign territory to you. Ben would not answer unwise questions but it could save you a little embarrassment if I warned you in advance. He's a snapper when he snaps. Believe you me.'

The stiffness went out of Mardie and her chin came back to normal. 'I'm sorry,' she said. 'I misunderstood you.'

'Of course you did. That's why I'm throwing out a few cautions. Most people new up here make mistakes. Isn't that so, Mrs Richie? It's better to be warned in advance.'

Mrs Richie looked from one girl to the other. 'Of course they do, Miss Seddon,' she agreed. 'But we don't make that kind of mistake at The Breakaway. We'd never survive on this corner if we were a source of gossip, or acted as informants about our customers. Very careful about that sort of thing is what we have to be.'

She turned her back while she returned the hot water jug to its proper place then gathered together the cups and saucers.

Her hands full of china, she departed – head up, forward march – through the door ahead of Mardie. Her manner truly matriarchal.

It was Mardie's turn to look at the other girl with raised eyebrows.

Joanna laughed. When she did this her whole expression changed to something really attractive. Mardie laughed too.

'She's a wonder, she is!' she said, meaning Mrs Richie. 'I'm glad you are not offended. After all, the Dig-in . . . which means you at the moment . . . is our customer too.'

'I'm not in the least bit offended. I like plain talking. You might have noticed that, Mardie. I make a thing of it myself, but I like to choose my time and place. Remember

I have to stop being female and become a *person* – something quite different – when I'm out at the camp. You asked me how I managed with all those men. Well, now you know.'

'I'd like to change places with you one day. It must be fun. Sort-of playing two parts.'

'Yes, but not at the same time. Well, come on . . .' She lifted herself with her marked athletic ease from the chair. 'Let's go and see if Mrs Richie, in her own indomitable fashion, has now managed to quell Ben's appetite for beer and food. There's loading-up to be done.'

Time passed and Mardie heard no more from the Dig-in over the closed circuit. Occasionally she could pick them up talking on the open transceiver service to which all the people in the outback listened and talked on during the Open Session. The news of the day was whirled around the sound waves high above Mother Earth from homestead to homestead. And occasionally from exploration camp to exploration camp, giving friendly news but never business or geological facts.

A contractor had come up from the south to see Mardie about quoting for the erection of her accommodation section. This was to be built as motel-type units and along the north boundary. Mr Lawson had sent this particular contractor, which meant that he, Mr Lawson, was supporting Mardie in her project after all. He wrote that he had been impressed by Mardie's determination but more so by her neat costing figures. Clearly she had done her homework and done it very well.

Light planes came and went on the landing ground across the bitumen. Trucks, cars, utilities, low-loaders, carrying mine-making equipment for every kind of ore body from iron to nickel north of Twenty-six, passed up and down the road from day to day. Sometimes there were no more than two vehicles a day. At other times there could be as many as a dozen through-travellers. They all stopped. They all bought something . . . and Mardie had grown to love them. Each time someone came in it was like meeting people from Mars . . . they had come such incredible distances, and yet had incredible distances to go. For them The Breakaway was what it was – an oasis in the desert, a haven – and they said so. 'A God-send' they called the place. Mardie intended to improve on that. Soon really weary travellers from as far out as the Gibson

Desert or as far north as the Kimberley's could get a night's rest. She meant to make it a real stop-over. Real motel units. She hoped – in some other world, wherever he was – that her godfather was looking down and approving.

'When I first came up here,' Mardie said one day as she helped Mrs Richie polish the brasses, 'a man driving through said that "nothing ever happens here in the outback." Now just look what *is* happening! The Breakaway could be Main Street on Thursday. We even polish the already polished brasses because the workmen are arriving to put in the foundations for my "Motel".'

'Be thankful for an early start, Mardie. And I like the brass to shine all the time.'

'Of course you do. Me too. I was thinking how flat-out busy we are. First the contractor, then Mister Falldown coming in with little injured Doggie. Next we had the store truck arriving from down south and the men camping overnight at the back. Now the Flying Vet is arriving. Mr Richie said The Breakaway will be full. All the people coming in from the far reaches of the Never with their pet dogs, cats, kangaroos and parrots to see the Vet will call in here. It will be like a real party.'

'Oh! We'll make time for you to go to the Vet with Doggie. No owner seems to have come back to claim the poor little thing, so as we don't look like parting with him, we'd better give him a proper name.'

'Let's call him after Mister Falldown. So appropriate. If Mister Falldown hadn't once had a fall and lost his memory we wouldn't have him living out there in the bush all alone, would we? He said Doggie would have fallen off someone's truck.'

'Which reminds me, Mister's due in for stores on the last day of every month, Mardie. That's next Tuesday. Mark it on the calendar with the red pencil, will you, dear? The police from North Port always radio in an inquiry the day after he's due.'

Mardie went to the wall behind the bar counter. She put a large red ring round the Tuesday.

'It seems silly the North-west police asking about anyone so harmless,' Mardie said a little sadly. 'He walked all those miles to bring Doggie in – just in case its owner turned up again.'

'Which its owner hasn't done. Well, Mister will tell us if

we can keep the dog when he comes in for the stores. The police only want to know if he's all right. That's why they radio. All those miles out in the bush – on his own – he could be ill or even dead before anyone knew. The police just check for his own good. If no one heard from Mister they'd go out to see if he's all right.'

'Yes, I know. Fifteen miles out there in the bush *alone.* It seems so strange, doesn't it? I minded being alone before I came up here, yet I lived in a city suburb in a house with two other people.'

'You just felt you didn't belong. That's the difference. Mister Falldown belongs in the bush. He knows every stick of mulga and every stone, insect, kangaroo, emu, lizard, parrot – you name it – for a hundred miles around. He's not alone. He's where he wants to be – with the bush. That's life to him and the only kind he knows. He was born out there in the first rush of the goldfields days. Everyone else dead and gone. But he stays on. He's done no harm to anyone and . . .'

'Does a lot of good. Like bringing in poor injured Doggie.'

'Last time it was one of those explorers. Lost his way, did that one, and didn't do what he should have done – which was stay with his Land-Rover. Started off to walk in circles after the sun got him. Twenty-four hours is all you can last in that heat without water. Even the steep drop in temperature at night won't save someone wandering.'

'How often does that happen?'

'Now and again. Last time it was a year or two back. Some Smart Alec set off from North Port with his wife and three kids. He took a new turn just because the track looked a better one. This new track had been made by oil explorers. They'd abandoned it. If he'd kept going, he'd have found it went nowhere but the Gibson Desert. Two aborigines went after that car because they saw new tracks, and knew it was all wrong. That feller and his whole family owe their lives to those two aborigines.'

'I hope they realized it and showed they were grateful,' Mardie said warmly.

'They would have if they could. The two abos didn't wait for any thanks after they brought them back as far as the right turning. They just disappeared in the bush again like they'd never been out of it.'

Mardie, back at the polishing, paused at her rubbing. 'It must be terrifying to be lost out there in that wilderness,' she said thoughtfully.

It was hot right now, but she felt a shiver run down her spine. Yet at night, in some seasons, the temperature could drop almost to freezing. Strange, strange land!

She didn't believe in premonitions, let alone somebody's classic proverb about 'events casting their shadows before'. She shrugged off the uncomfortable feeling.

'Well,' she said, after a long pause, 'shall we call Doggie "Digger"? He'll have to have a name and address for the Vet.'

' "Digger". I like the sound of it. Besides, it gives him a kind of purpose. That's what they called the miners in the early days. That's why the soldiers, when the war came, were called "diggers". He's a very dignified little doggie, isn't he? I mean, the way he holds up his head, sideways sort-of. Nothing hang-dog. And his leg must have caused him a lot of pain.'

'That's why he licks it all the time. It's a dog's way of curing sores. Something in the spittle has curing properties.'

'But it won't cure a broken bone, if it *is* broken. I can't get to the Flying Vet quick enough to find out.'

When finally the news came over the transceiver as to the exact time and place of the Vet's landing, Mardie set off with the little, half-grown blue-heeler in The Breakaway's utility. The Vet was landing by the cross-tracks thirty miles up the bitumen.

'Glad to see you have your survival kit in the back, Mardie,' Mr Richie said. 'Got the lot? Water, petrol, spade, shovel, crossbars? Food for girl and dog?'

'Yes. And my wrist-watch in case I lose the compass.' Mardie started up the engine and smiled back at her mentor.

Survival kits she knew weren't a joke. Every police station provided the list free. But, after all, her journey was only up the bitumen and back. No cross-country tracks for her. Still, survival kits were regulation – so she had one. Even though Mansell's out-paddock where the Vet was landing had its west boundary bang on this same bitumen.

'Mr Richie,' she called through the window, 'you didn't mention the shade hat. I have the "custom of the country" one on the seat beside me.'

'Which one's that?'

'Like Joanna Seddon's hat. The same as the one Jard Hunter wears. And those other explorer types we see going through.'

'Listen, love. Don't you go exploring now. You stick around

the Vet. No taking a walk in the bush to stretch your legs. Mansell Station is a million acres. You try looking for their homestead, or some such, you'll need Mister Falldown or a couple of aborigines to find you.'

'I won't . . . unless I'm asked and someone takes me. I heard on the transceiver someone from Mansell is taking a kelpie sheep dog to the Vet. Who knows? I just might be invited.'

'Good luck if you do. They're a nice lot out there. But don't forget to let us know.'

'I'll let you know. Don't *you* forget to listen to the Session in case there's a message.'

'We won't. Off you go, lass. Bring us back all the news. And give us some warning about how many of those Vet visitors are likely to come down later to The Breakaway for a drink and tucker.'

'Of course. I won't forget.'

'By the way, Jard Hunter will be there. He always gets there when the Vet comes in. I've never known him miss. He's an old schoolfriend or something. If you do go to the Mansell homestead he can call us on his two-way.'

'Will do!' Mardie hardly knew she said it. The name Jard Hunter did something to her adrenalin – and not for the reasons Joanna Seddon had suggested. It was just this strange feeling about the man.

Anyway, she thought, as she speeded northwards, it's something extra interesting to look forward to on this trip.

Who said nothing ever happens in the outback!

FIVE

The miles flew by. The scenery on either side did not change one whit. Miles and miles to east and west scattered mulga stood in clumps. In the distance, far to the north-east, lay the haze of mesa mountains. She could have been standing still outside The Breakaway for all the difference there was in the land. One gets the feeling, she thought, that this is the whole world for ever and ever. So empty!

No wonder people get lost.

Then unexpectedly the scene did change – just that little bit. The ribbon of bitumen wasn't straight any more. There was a curve coming up.

A quarter of a mile round the curve a fence stretched across the land from east to west, except for a gap where the road ran over a sheep grid. At this point, she knew, Mansell Station began. The bitumen was actually running through its property.

Round another curve she came upon that wonder thing – *humanity* again.

Fifty yards on the east side of the road were – quite literally – *people.* And trees! They were white-trunked shady gum trees like those along the boundary at The Breakaway. Under these trees were perhaps twenty people sitting on boulders, or bush rugs. They were grouped round a landed plane which was the same size, and had the look of the Flying Doctor's ambulance. It was a white plane with an insignia painted on its side above the large printed name *Flying Veterinary Service.*

A man in a white coat was standing by a camp table examining a small animal on it. Beside him was a girl in a white coat handing him swabs.

Each and all of the people sitting about held some kind of animal or bird in their arms, or in cages, cat baskets, or on leashes.

Cars and utilities were scattered around on the paddock verge like large pieces of technological litter. The largest was a truck, on the tray of which stood a bull with a ring through its nose. A man sitting on the side of the truck was holding a rod tethered to the ring.

'Of all things . . .' Mardie said to herself as she swung the utility in and became part of the motor litter. She braked to a stop. She was staring at the bull – the largest she had ever seen or dreamed possible. The most interesting thing about it was not the ring in its nose but a hump on its back just behind the shoulders. A brahmin bull!

The people sitting around, one and all, turned to look at the newcomer. Mardie scanned each face eagerly.

No. Jard Hunter was not there. She wondered why she felt disappointed.

Oh well! If Mr Richie hadn't mentioned it she wouldn't have thought of that mystery geologist . . . Beg pardon. Hydro-geologist.

As she lifted the small dog out of the utility she had one further thought: Well! He ought to be here. Those trees mean underground water, and he's interested in water.

She turned with her bundle and saw a small speck high

in the sky coming over a distant, thick, bushy area near the mesa mountains. She stood still, the dog in her arms like a cradled baby, and watched that speck grow larger, then become a clacking sound and finally turn out to be a small helicopter.

Perhaps it's him . . .

It was, but Mardie was not sure of that until after the helicopter landed and the tall slim man – cotton flopper still shading his face – came in his slow but steady tread towards the Vet's plane. He, too, was carrying a small brown animal in his arms, its head peering out from a sugar bag.

No one greeted him. Mardie wondered if it was because no one but herself knew who he was.

Then a man did speak up. 'For crying out loud!' he said in shocked tones. 'He's carrying a ruddy *dingo pup*.'

'He'd better keep it in that sugar bag and sit on it before someone ups and shoots it,' another man said. 'They're killers, those things. I'd like to see him let that one loose in my sheep pen. I'd be reaching for my gun. Damn quick at that!'

'But you can train them in a way.'

'I'll believe that when I see it.'

They'd all said 'hallo' to Mardie and she had smiled back. Now she spoke for the first time.

'Perhaps he intends to *try*. To train it, I mean. It is worth trying, isn't it? It's a lovely looking pup.'

'So is the enemy's eye in the sights of a bren gun,' the first speaker said caustically. Obviously he did not like dingoes – the wild dog of Australia.

Jard Hunter gave no sign that he knew either he or his bundle were matters of interest. He sat down under the shade of the plane's wing and held the sugar bag, pup-laden, in his arms. His eyes moved round the waiting group. One or two of the women essayed a tentative smile of welcome but his own mouth barely moved. Then he saw Mardie on the far side of the circle.

'Hallo,' she said brightly, making the best of her best smile.

He half-lifted his hat, smiled, but said nothing.

Was he shy? Or just plain unfriendly? she wondered. Well, she would put it to the test.

She stood up, walked round behind the group, and sat down beside him. 'Remember me? I'm Mardie Forrester from The Breakaway.'

'Yes. I remember you, Miss Forrester. We have something

in common. We share a city solicitor, I believe.'

'Mr Lawson. Actually he was my godfather's solicitor, and still looks after the estate.'

He really smiled this time. It did something to Mardie's heart, but she wanted to feel annoyed about that. And couldn't.

She turned away and looked at the helicopter sitting on the ground like some large, extraordinary, top-heavy spider.

'I've never been in a helicopter,' she said. She had to say something to get rid of that strange feeling she had.

That thing called 'falling in love'? Oh, please *not*!

Her father and his new wife. She had had to run away from it because it was something they had to pretend to hide. They had feared she wouldn't understand. Or might resent, because she had lost her own mother. She had to give them a chance all on account of this thing called *love*.

Other people had it. But not herself.

She had had her boy-friends . . . the same as other girls. That was before her mother became ill. A little flirtation here and a little flirtation there. But her heart had not turned over. Sometimes in the loneliness of a lonely night she had wondered. What was it really like? Would it ever come her way? Would she miss out?

Now, here on the edge of a sheep station which was a million acres because it was so near semi-desert it took a whole acre to feed one sheep, her heart had turned, well . . . not quite over, but nearly. This, because of a man with a touch of mystery about his work and a veil of reserve, perhaps even mystery too, about his manner. Someone to whom she had spoken but once before. How silly could she get?

'A helicopter . . .' she said once again, vaguely. 'Last time it was a utility.'

'Next time it could be an aeroplane. I can manage all three . . .' His smile was still there and he was watching Mardie's face as if he, too, wondered a little about *her*.

But he belonged to Joanna, didn't he? Or did he?

'Do you ever take girl passengers?' she asked, still not looking at him. 'I mean people like Joanna Seddon from out at the Dig-in?'

'Oh yes. She can all but fly it herself, except she hasn't yet got her licence. I've been teaching her.'

This time she did look at him.

'But you are at the out-camp. I suppose with a helicopter and a Company aeroplane you can jump across to see anyone you like whenever you want to.'

'Well, it's not as easy as that. One has other things to do.'

'Other things to do?'

'Yes,' he said. 'And not always to do with water.'

Mardie looked down at Digger and patted his head.

Not always to do with water could mean a lot to do with 'courting'. That would take time too.

'What's wrong with your dog?' he asked her. 'He's a newcomer to The Breakaway, isn't he?'

'Yes. Mister Falldown – the bush hermit – brought him in a week ago. He thinks the poor little thing must have fallen off a truck and been left behind. We're not sure whether his leg is broken or not. It's painful and it creaks when we've tried to examine it. Your patient is a dingo pup, isn't it? Aren't dingoes dreaded in sheep country?'

'Some say yes. The conservationists say no. He has one thing in common with your dog. Mister Falldown had him in his camp. He's had a foot caught in a trap.'

'Mister Falldown?' Mardie was surprised. 'Why, that's one friend we have in common. He loves animals, wild or tame, doesn't he?'

'Yes. He lives with them. You name the animal – he has it. Not least a herd of self-reared goats, a wild donkey, and – believe this one or not – a baby camel, likewise rescued injured out in the scrub south of the mesas.'

'He must have a positive zoo out there in the bush.'

'That place he lives in, Miss Forrester, has to be seen to be believed. For all he can speak his variety of English when he wants to, he mostly speaks the language of the animals or that of his own people. He's a descendant partly from the aborigines and partly from the old Afghan camel-drivers of the early days.'

'We call this doggie "Digger". When Mister brought him in he – Mister Falldown – didn't seem to be able to speak English at all. Mrs Richie said it was because he hadn't been in touch for ages, and sometimes he forgets how.'

Jard Hunter nodded his head. 'Same with me when I dropped down the other day. By the time I left, his English was coming back good and strong. It all depends on his mood.'

'Dropped down? You mean in the helicopter?'

'Yes. I was above that way and dropped down to see if the old codger was all right. That's when he gave me this pup to bring to the Vet.'

'The police ask The Breakaway about him over the air,'

Mardie said. 'I don't suppose Mister Falldown knows, but it's really for his own good. If he doesn't come in for his stores they'd know he was ill . . . or that something had happened to him.'

Jard Hunter pulled his hat down, shadowing his face again as he looked out over the low scrub bush and mulga plains into the miles and miles of the Never country.

'He'd know they put a call out about him, Mardie,' he said slowly, his drawl much more pronounced. 'You don't mind me calling you Mardie?'

'Oh no! Everyone, even the truckies, call me by my given name.'

'Old Mister probably knows more about everything, in his own fashion, than all the rest of us put together,' Jard went on after a small, thoughtful kind of silence.

'About helicopters, for instance?'

'Certainly. If I'm heading that way he knows hours before I know myself that I'm going to land and see how he and his menagerie are getting on.'

Mardie laughed. 'I almost believe you,' she said.

Jard looked at her. 'You'd better,' he said quite seriously. 'Nobody this side of heaven knows how Mister Falldown *knows*. He just does.'

Mardie shook her head as if in wonder. She had heard about people like old Mister Falldown – lost memory and all – but it was hard to understand, let alone accept that a lone bushman who had never been to school, never seen civilization other than a stop-over like The Breakaway, should know so much. He'd learned bush lore from his forebears, she supposed.

'I went to school,' she said, after quite a silence. 'And afterwards I learned book-keeping and typing, yet I don't know anything about a helicopter except what I see sitting over there.'

Jard glanced at her again. The slow smile touched his face unexpectedly, giving it an almost gentle look. It stirred Mardie's heart again. She didn't know whether it was with pain or delight. Oh, *why* did he have this effect on her? Actually she wanted *not to like him*. Or didn't she?

'Would you like to try one from the inside?' he asked, more curious, she thought, to see her reaction than really meaning it.

Her face lit up. 'Oh yes. Please! Would you? I mean, would you really take me up?'

'Certainly. That is, after the Vet has attended to our invalids.

Would you like a run over the Dig-in, to see it from a heavenly angle?'

'I'd love that. I've wanted to see it ever so badly. Ever since . . .'

His eyebrows were raised. 'Ever since what?'

'Since Joanna Seddon came in with the truck to The Breakaway. She told me a little about it.'

'Ah, Joanna!' he said, and looked away into the distance as if his thoughts had gone elsewhere. He was no longer with her. His face had that shadowed, tidied-away look again.

Joanna means a lot to him, Mardie thought, as she bent her head and patted the small dog on her lap.

The Vet's assistant was beckoning to her.

'Excuse me,' Mardie said. 'I think it must be my turn.'

He half stood as she left him. Just politeness, she admitted. She feared he wasn't really noticing that she was leaving his side.

'The dog's name and address, please,' the girl said professionally, getting ready to fill in a card. The card was just the same as a nurse uses in a doctor's surgery, and there was a file standing waiting on the small camp table beside her. Presently the card would be neatly packed into it, just as for human patients in a hospital.

'His name's Digger.'

'Oh really . . .' the receptionist said, pulling in the corners of her mouth. 'We have too many "Diggers".' She looked Mardie straight in the eyes as if to reprimand her. 'This is one of Mr Falldown's rescues, isn't it? Actually that man needs a Vet to himself. Couldn't you please give the dog another name?'

'Well,' Mardie said. 'If I must. Um . . . let me think. "Mister-Digger". Yes, I'll call him that. If they call the runners out at the Dig-in Diggers there wouldn't be one of them with a double-barrelled name, would there. It's sort of aristocratic.'

The girl looked up quickly. 'You mean the Exploration Company? Oh, you know them out there, do you?' She began busily filling in the card. 'What are they finding out there now, do you suppose? So interesting . . .'

'I don't know,' Mardie said. 'I haven't asked. I thought it wasn't done . . . *to ask.* That is . . .'

The girl gave a wry smile. 'Well, if you haven't asked you're the only one this side of the black stump so incurious. All the same, if you *do* hear anything, you will let us know, won't you?'

'His . . . I mean the dog's address is The Breakaway,' Mardie said.

'Oh dear. I wish you'd said so at first. Now I'm making a mess of this card. I'd better do another.'

Mardie stood in silence while the rest of the formalities took place. She watched as the new card was ceremoniously filled in.

Name Mister-Digger.

Address The Breakaway.

Owner Mister Falldown.

Owner's address Somewhere in the bush.

Complaint Suspected broken right hind leg.

'That will do for the moment,' the girl said briefly. 'Now if you would sit down with the patient on the other side of that lady with the white cat, over there. It will be your turn after her.'

'Thank you.' Mardie spoke so meekly she didn't recognize herself. It was exactly like registering in the Out-Patients at a city hospital. The 'nurse' – if that was what the assistant was called – was almost as impersonal and nearly as formidable as some officials in a hospital could be.

Mardie regretted having to sit by the woman with the white cat but only because she could not go back and sit by Jard Hunter. He might forget he had said he would take her up in the helicopter. He just could be the absent-minded kind from that quiet, faraway expression that seemed to spend most of its time shadowing his face.

Her regrets were later dispelled. The little group in which she found herself was suddenly and quite wonderfully in a world of its own. The conversation was full of chat and gossip. All kindly. Some of it laughter-making. It's a wonderful thing to hear laughter, Mardie thought wistfully. And that led her to thinking of David Ashton, and his jokes over the air.

Each person sitting there related to the others the story of his or her animal. It was a good mouser, this one. It was kept in the storeroom. 'And let any other cat dare stick its nose in her preserves!' This one's dog never barked, never bit, but it never let anyone or anything pass it either. 'It has such a ferocious look, see. That's why. But it's as harmless as a baby. That lady over there, see? She can't sit here with her cat – not because any of these dogs take any notice.

They're used to cats. But *that* cat doesn't like dogs . . . What a cheek! The silly striped hyena – not to like dogs! A tabby. Has to sit apart as if it's queen pin, or something.

'And see that bloke with the sheep? You wouldn't believe it but he runs thirty thousand sheep on his station, but that one has to be brought in to the Vet. It was reared as a pet lamb, that's why. Even when it runs with the mob it always lags behind the others and remembers the boss. It gets wind-grass clogging up its knees, like most of the others at this time of the year. But *it's* the one that has to be brought in to the Vet. Not the other twenty-nine and some thousand. That feller over there past the aeroplane – he's a horse-breaker. Cruel hard those horse-breakers can be sometimes, but let his own nag get a stake through its leg and boy, is he in a state! He's in here to see the Vet like it's the only animal in the world that counts.'

Mardie found it enthralling.

They talked of their animals much more than any row of worried mothers talked about their babies in a doctor's waiting-room. With much more energy too. Everyone had a story to tell about his or her animal.

Before Mardie knew what she was doing, she, too, was telling them about her own protégé – where it came from, what she feared was wrong with it, and what a darling little pet it was.

'Ought to be shot – those truck drivers,' one man said. 'The way they boom down that bitumen at top speed with a dog sitting out on the tailboard. Don't know why the RSPCA doesn't do something about it. One of these days I'll write a letter to the paper about them.'

Each and all nodded heads and agreed.

'It's a good job Mister Falldown found the poor little fellow,' the woman with the white cat confided to Mardie. 'We all know about *him* – meaning Mister Falldown. Quite a character in the district, he is. Miles out there in the bush on his own. Not that I've ever seen him myself. But we all know about him. One day every month the police come over the transceiver asking news of him. If any of the stockmen have seen him they report in. Just to tell he's all right and not sick or dying or something.'

Mardie nodded. She was brought right in by this serious conversation, and was one of them.

'Yes, I know,' she said. 'They call The Breakaway because he comes in for stores, and they want to know if he's been in at his usual time. They really *care* about him, don't they?'

'Oh-h-h! You're the new girl at The Breakaway? We've all heard about you. You're going to put up some motel-type sleep-overs they say. You look too young to be taking on something big like that.'

'Perhaps I'm older than I look,' Mardie said wryly.

'Aren't you lonely along there just with the Richies?'

'No. I was lonely before I came. Now I have The Breakaway. And the Richies.'

'And your doggie, of course. What did you say you've called him?'

'Mister-Digger, hyphenated. That is . . . since ten minutes ago. The Vet's assistant wouldn't let me call him just Digger. But I'll leave off the "Mister" when I get home.'

There was a general laugh all round.

'Should think not – ' one man said firmly, but quite kindly. 'There's everything under the sun from emus, kangaroos to dingoes called something after that old bushwhacker. All because the old bushy won't bring them in himself. Always finds someone else to do the job. The girl over there must have given up arguing with you if she let you leave the "Mister" in along with "Digger".'

Mardie nodded her head in the plane's direction where Jard Hunter was sitting under its wing-shade.

'Jard Hunter sitting over there has brought the dingo pup in for Mister Falldown,' she said.

SIX

To her surprise a sudden silence fell on the group.

'Hm . . .' someone said at length. 'So that's Jard Hunter, is it? I've been wondering. Keeps to himself, doesn't he? We've heard about *him*.'

'Oh no. Not really – ' Mardie found herself leaping to Jard Hunter's defence. 'He's really very nice. He's come to The Breakaway several times. I think you have to get to know him. It's just that he's the strong silent kind, I think.'

One man on the other side of the ring, holding a sheep dog, was suddenly looking at Mardie closely. 'You were over there talking to him, weren't you? What does he talk about anyway? What they're doing out there at the Dig-in?'

'Oh no,' Mardie said quickly. 'We were talking about the helicopter. And Mister Falldown.'

A woman with a striped ginger cat in a basket laughed. 'Well . . . if he ever does talk about what they find out there . . . beside who's who with that girl who seems to run them all . . . you'll let us in on the know, won't you? They've pegged half of our station as mineral claims so we're entitled to be in on it if they make a good strike.'

The animals were suddenly forgotten and for the next ten minutes Mardie heard more about companies pegging claims on other people's stations, of nickel strikes, and of oil finds than she'd dreamed possible. The newspapers had been full of it for months, of course, but it had been something over her head. Now she learned for the first time that, when you owned a sheep station, you only owned what grew or was placed on the top nine inches of the soil. Anyone could peg a claim to explore what was *under* the ground, provided the Warden's Court agreed the applicants were the first to claim and were not over-pegging someone else's claim.

'The big lurk,' one man explained – in between talking to his pair of caged cockatoos – 'is when the night raiders move in and shift the pegs a mile or two off and put their own pegs in. You can't map your claim in *miles* in these areas. You have to map by taking bearings from some permanent landmark like Dead Man's Well or Mount Best Mesa. Half the Warden's time is taken up settling rows over who claimed what and where, first.'

'The place seems to have gone mineral mad,' Mardie said, shaking her head doubtfully.

'Well, when there's a mining boom on, that's it! It was the same in the big gold-prospecting days. That's how The Breakaway came out. It built up out of nowhere to service the gold prospectors. Same as now, I guess, some of your best customers are the nickel and oil boys. Eh?'

Yes, Mardie had to agree to that, but she was careful to be tactful how she acknowledged it. These people attending the Vet's session were mostly station people and they, too, were possibly Breakaway's customers at some time or other. She hadn't asked their names, so wasn't able to equate them with her account books.

The brown cotton flop hat – and the helicopter – had given Jard Hunter's occupation away. Perhaps it was for that reason he sat apart from the others over there under the shade of the plane's wing. He and these pastoralists were almost natural enemies unless he – with the possibility of inside information – let them in on the chance to buy shares if the Dig-in made a really rich strike.

But it's a marvellous world outback, all the same! she thought to herself. She hadn't dreamed, so alone back there in the city, that anything in the outback could be such fun – with so much friendly *talk* – as this gathering 'at the Vet's' on the corner of a million-acre paddock! All rather wonderful.

Specially as presently Jard Hunter might take her for a ride in that helicopter.

The invalid animals and birds, one by one, were attended to by the Vet. Even the bull, which like one or two other animals had been staked, had had his attention. Mr Falldown's doggie – now Mister-Digger – had a lengthwise crack in his hind leg and not a cross break. So the Vet pinned it, then bound it.

'Watch the binding and keep it on for three days, then change it,' he advised. 'If I splint it he'll gnaw the splints away. Even break them off. This way he won't worry it. If you keep a watch on the binding the bone will mend itself, given time.' He gave Mardie an extra plastic package of the special kind of binding used. There was no cost, which surprised her very much. The Veterinary Service was a voluntary one supported by a rich endowment from a group of wealthy pastoralists.

'If there's a war on between pastoralists and explorers,' Mardie said to Jard later as he helped her up into the helicopter, 'I'm temporarily on the side of the pastoralists. They care about animals, don't they?'

'Some of them,' he replied cryptically. He strapped her in, then strapped himself. His eyes caught hers, and again he wore that slow half-smile that was so puzzling. 'One and all of them sitting there would have taken a pot shot at the dingo pup if they'd had a chance,' he finished.

'Why do you care about it then? They are killers, the dingoes, aren't they?'

'Nasty killers if you don't guard your sheep.'

'Then why did you bring him to the Vet?'

'Because he's Mister Falldown's pup. And he asked me to bring him in. Moreover – killers or not – they're magnificent dogs, as wild dogs go.'

'It's as simple as that?'

'As simple as that.'

Strange, strange! Mardie thought. He cares about Mister Falldown. Like the police care about him. And all the other people know about him and perhaps, in their own way, care about him too! A brown-black hermit in the bush. Yet they *cared*. It was a good world – this outback!

Funny, but she too, and the Richies, cared about Mister Falldown. There must be good in human nature after all.

'In fact, it's all very remarkable,' she said aloud. Jard did not hear her because they were lifting and the wind the 'copter made was swishing a wild circle all around as they left the ground. It made a grizzly grinding noise too. When this noise faded out into a routine engine sound Jard was speaking on his two-way to someone somewhere else, perhaps miles and miles away across the stony semi-desert, and island stretches of bushland.

She could not hear what he was saying because he spoke into a tiny tube hung to his neck. When he had finished he glanced at her again.

'What's it feel like to be a bird?' he asked. He had a smile in his eyes.

'Wonderful. Here am I flying in the sky. Sort-of hovering, and wind-borne like a bird. It's different from flying in a plane, isn't it?'

'Exactly. In a plane you think you're standing still in the air and it's the ground underneath that's moving. In a helicopter you know it's you who's flying.'

'It's good of you to take me.' Mardie looked at him curiously. 'Why are you taking me, Jard? I may call you Jard?'

'Yes. I call you Mardie, don't I? Fair exchange. Call me Jard. Why am I taking you? Because I thought you might like to come.

'It's as simple as that?'

'Simple as that.'

They both laughed. That word 'simple' was becoming routine speech between them.

He had a beautiful shining look about his face when he laughed. Mardie wondered why – in a way – it made her feel sad as well as glad. Something gained? Something lost? A friend for a moment. When that moment was gone – what next?

The whirligig blades above them carried them over the mulga and stony ground. Then over freaked-out lines that scored and broke the manilla-brown earth like long or short fissures in a moon world. In fact like one of the moon walkers had said – 'Magnificent desolation'. Later they hovered across a wide stretch of low scrubland. Next they were ascending – up, up and up. They were nearing the mesas.

These flat-topped mountains were green all over where everywhere else had been brown. Up and down and angle-wise across the mesa sides were wide rude gashes, leaving the iron-red boulder-strewn soil like weals wide-striped across the living green of the low spinifex grass and scrub.

'Costeans,' Jard explained. 'Those are long trenches made by the Exploration Company, using the dragline dredges to break the surface so that the mesas will yield up their mineral secrets – *if any.*'

'If any? Yet there's no one there. Nobody in sight.'

'No surface indications of mineralization either. You may say they were a "no-find". Such an explicit description *that.* So the dragline has gone elsewhere. You'll see it presently when we cross over.'

'And it leaves behind those great hideous gashes to spoil the range.'

'A mountain range is not a living thing in the same way as your Digger or Mister Falldown's dingo pup, Mardie.'

'But it's not a dead thing either. Trees and bush scrub and grass are living . . .'

'Exactly. They will grow again. Not this season, but maybe next. The scars will cover up. You have to be realistic if you live in this part of the world. Minerals mean wealth and wealth means schools, hospitals, homes for the poor as well as the rich.'

Jard suddenly pushed his hat to the back of his head and looked obliquely up at the sky. He narrowed his eyes, seeing something Mardie herself could not see.

'Talking about living things,' he said ominously, 'there's a couple of wedge-tailed eages up there.'

'Where? I can't see them.'

'Your sight is not used to looking into distances. But they're there, and they're not a helicopter's best friend.'

'Why?'

'They follow and hang around. They have a nuisance value – and that's all.'

Mardie's spirits dropped just that fraction. She didn't want Jard to think this way – sort-of callous about giant gashes in the sides of lovely mountains, and almost murderous about wide-winged wild birds just because they 'hung around'. Why were they a nuisance? They were huge birds she knew but not all *that* big. That is, they couldn't damage a metal monster like a helicopter, could they?

Minutes later they were flying over the Dig-in's encampment.

'There! Coming up on your port side, Mardie. Those white dots spilled along the base – east side of the east mesa.'

The white dots became small rectangular camp huts. Bunk houses they called them. Some were larger than others. They stood in an irregular line. Further along eastwards was a drilling rig – a giant piece out of a Meccano set. It was clearly being worked, for there were men down there, watching something being hoist upwards towards a platform on which stood more men.

Those small earth-bound beings had heard, then seen the helicopter. Some of them waved their hats, then set them firmly back on their heads and went on with their work. Nearby, smoke was puffing lazily upwards from yet another, larger, white hut.

'Where do you suppose Joanna is?' Mardie asked lightly. 'In the cook house or on the rig.'

'Neither,' Jard replied laconically. 'She's out along the strike line today, I imagine. Her jeep's missing. The gossan her team is working on runs crosswise between those two rises to the west.'

There were, down there, a number of jeeps standing about. *He'd looked for hers and noticed it was gone.* Somewhere in those low hills Joanna – being in her geologist rôle today – would have heard the 'copter and perhaps would be looking upwards to catch sight of it. They were flying low so that Mardie could see the details of the encampment and wherever Joanna was she might see who was Jard's passenger. Would she mind?

Mardie remembered that sharp, upwards glance and the firm statement Joanna had made the day she had come to The Breakaway. What was hers was hers. So hands off. It hadn't been in those words but that was what she had meant.

'I'm glad I've seen it,' Mardie said as the 'copter swung away and gained height again. 'Thank you so much for bringing me. Do you think we'd better turn back to the cross-roads again? I've thirty miles to drive back and the Richies might begin to get anxious.'

Jard's slow smile was at work again. 'You can't get lost on the bitumen, Mardie,' he said. 'And the Richies know that. It's people who take to the bush tracks who strike trouble.'

'Not people who take to helicopters?' Mardie asked with a laugh.

'Well, you would come.'

'Well, you would ask me.'

He glanced sideways at her.

'Do you always go where you're asked? Is it a habit of yours?'

Mardie was leaning sideways watching the ground – the patches of spinifex here and there, the odd claypans that made picturesque patterns laid out like a psychedelic map of strange shapes. Then she saw the kangaroos.

'Look . . . for heaven's sake!' she exclaimed. 'There must be thousands of them.' They were, from this height, little grey animals, not thousands but hundreds of them racing through the bush and over the spinifex in a bob-hopping way – all streaming off in the one direction. Then, on the other side of the 'copter, she could see the emus. Not so many of them but still scores. They seemed to keep in line with the helicopter as if, from their lowly earth-bound situation, they were racing this big sky bird.

'That's just what they are doing,' Jard explained. 'They have a mental attitude to speed. If anything's going fast they'll go faster. It's a way of life with them.'

'But where are they all going? And those hundreds of kangaroos? Are they scared by the 'copter?'

Jard shrugged. 'Could be. More likely they've eaten out their last paddock and are off to eat out the next one.'

'You are *not* a conservationist, are you,' Mardie said accusingly. 'I don't think you feel anything for those creatures down there.'

'I do,' he said bluntly. 'I also feel for the thousands of dead sheep lying around after the drought. Who does the eating? The kangaroos or the sheep, Mardie? And who makes the choice?'

She sat back and thought. Her face was sad because she thought they *all* should eat. Choice? She was glad it was not hers to make.

There was quite a long silence between them. Then she noticed the sun had begun its westering course . . . way over her left shoulder.

'Where are we going now?' she asked, more to change the subject than anything else.

'Since this may be your only chance ever to take a ride in a 'copter, Mardie, I thought I'd take you a bit up northward so that you can see the one place round these parts where the underground water comes up in the kind of lake nobody has ever been able to explain. Below another line of mesas. You'll see thick bush there.'

'But that is your work, isn't it? Explaining underground water?'

'Oh, I can explain the water all right. But not what's growing round it. Palms. Dozens of them, and very beautiful. Palms are not indigenous to Australia. The riddle is . . . how did they get there?'

'Someone years ago planted them?'

He shook his head. 'Not out here in the nowhere. The earliest pioneers who went through here wrote about the palms in their diaries. No white people had ever been through here before.'

'Then brown people . . . from Asia?'

'Well, that's a theory, of course. But no other evidence of any kind or description has ever been found that Asians might at one time have inhabited the inland of Australia. That is before the blue eyes came with a Mr William Dampier, pirate, and a Captain Cook, Navy Officer.'

'The early Afghan camel-drivers?'

He shook his head again. 'They came after blue eyes, the white people. And for the white people – to carry their stores, goods and chattels.'

'Then it's a mystery?'

'Yes, but a beautiful one. Wait till you see them.'

He suddenly swung the helicopter to starboard, then straight ahead again. He said *'Damn'* in a forceful way.

Something was wrong. She sensed this, but did not ask. Jard's expression was one of complete concentration as he manoeuvred the machine to west, then east. Lessened height, then gained it.

Suddenly Mardie saw what it was he was trying to avoid. The huge eagles. Their wing span must have been yards wide, at least nine or ten feet anyway. They were rushing at and attacking the 'copter as if it was some deadly enemy.

A minute later it happened.

Jard had increased height to avoid one charge. They were over trees and thick bushland now. Then there come a shattering grinding thump. A terrible sound. The 'copter veered sideways and Mardie was thrown against Jard. His chin was down and he was working at the controls. An eagle slammed through the windscreen – its beak straight at Jard's head. There were feathers everywhere.

'Put your hands over your forehead, Mardie. Lean forward head down against the panel.' Jard seemed to speak in a mumble. *'NOW. Do as you're told.'*

Mardie obeyed. She leaned forward, her hands and arms protecting her forehead as she pressed it against the panel.

Some knowledge in her was crying out: *He can't protect himself. He has to keep at the controls. The eagle hit him. The windscreen's broken.*

He was bringing the 'copter down.

Then above – over the roof – came another terrible unearthly grinding sound. The 'copter ceased its quiet descent.

It fell.

She heard the windscreen smash as a tree branch broke through.

She was thrown about – this way, that.

Every bone in her body was shaken. Was she alive? Or dead?

Jard?

Her head whizzed.

I didn't see the palms after all. Then suddenly her mind went blank.

She couldn't think so she stared at Jard. He was slumped forwards, his head pinned down by the tree branch . . . and bleeding.

Seconds, minutes, she sat there. Or hours? Her mind wouldn't think.

But she must think. *She had to think.*

Was Jard dead?

Oh, please, dear God . . . *make me think*. Help me to *think*. I've always believed in You. Somewhere You . . .

The dizziness came over her again. She had to have will power . . .

The dizziness receded and slowly, inch by inch, she straightened up. No – her bones weren't broken. She moved her legs, her arms, her hands. Ever so gently she turned her head this way, then that.

She was talking to herself.

'Carefully, Mardie, carefully. You're alive so *you* have to be the one. It's up to you. Try yourself out. Your back? It's okay. It's up to you . . . if Jard is alive.'

SEVEN

Mardie never afterwards remembered how she did it. Inch by inch she tested her capacity to move. She put her hand on Jard's head. It was warm.

'Thank you, God, for that,' she said. 'Please excuse me if I don't say any more prayers just yet. I have to *think*. You see, he might be bleeding inside. Or have a broken neck. I have to think how to do it, I mean fix him up. You know . . . move him . . . you do understand, don't you?'

Mardie had never thought of herself as being friendly with God before. She hadn't even been sure whether He was someone up there, way out beyond other galaxies, or not. Or whether He was just a word for Goodness. She had settled for the fact that an ant would never understand a Diesel engine, let alone a Jumbo Jet aeroplane. So how could she, Mardie Forrester, understand about God? Or even try?

Now, suddenly, she was on friendly terms with Him. She was able to talk to Him . . . in between talking to and advising herself.

'Inch by inch, Mardie. Carefully now . . . If you're just Goodness . . . or maybe only Will Power . . . then stick around, won't you? I need you . . . because I'm the only one here. Well . . . there's Digger and Dingo Pup.'

There had to be the . . . well, what was it called?

'You know, the *gear* everyone had to take in case you were lost in the outback, or something – '

Every muscle and bone hurt but somehow she hefted herself into the rear end behind the seats. Yes. It was there. Shovel, trencher spade. Canned food, biscuits. An axe, but better – far, far better, a saw. And a First Aid Kit. Food and a can of water! A bush rug.

Her hands and arms were cut with broken pieces of windscreen and sharp tree spikes by the time she'd sawn that branch in two. Pain no longer mattered now because she had achievement.

'*There* you are. I told you so! *Will Power*!' She stopped and wondered: 'Who did I say that to?'

She talked and she worked. Sometimes she said rude things to Digger and Dingo Pup because they had too much to say for themselves. Digger had a marathon barking spree. Dingo Pup let out an unearthly howl every now and again.

She worked at getting the sawn branch free of the cabin. She thought kindness might be more effective with the animals, after all.

'There, there, my pets,' she said. 'I love you too and I'm glad you're alive . . . like Jard is. He's breathing but he's not kicking up your kind of racket about it because . . . you see . . . he's only *just* breathing.'

Somehow – and she thought it took hours, but wasn't sure – she got the tree branch out. Then, because Jard was freed, she pushed, pulled, dragged, prayed and finally at last had Jard out on the ground.

She didn't know whether or not helicopters could blow up because of spilt spirit the way aeroplanes could. But she thought not because the engine was stone cold now anyway. But she wouldn't take chances.

So inch by inch she pulled, pushed, drew Jard along the ground over low-growing bushes towards another grove of trees about a hundred yards away.

She bathed his head. 'Thank You up there for the can of water.' She felt Jard's pulse. She felt all his bones and every inch of his so dear body. It belonged to her now, didn't it? Because she was caring for it. She could find nothing *outwardly* wrong. Even his head didn't seem to have a crack in the cranium where the branch must have hit him when it came through the canopy. It was just as if he were asleep – only just breathing. Very pale.

Every now and again his body seemed seized with a rigor of shivering. Then he would lie still, as if dead. But he wasn't dead. He breathed – very shallow. And she could feel a faint but even pulse.

He was alive. She had this strange feeling about him being *hers*. Belonging.

Funny, when you have to care for someone . . . when they're totally dependent on you . . . that somebody becomes your own. Your very own. Like no one on earth had ever been like that before.

Her mother had belonged to everybody. So had her father . . . specially to his new wife. Only she, Mardie, had been alone in the sense that no one really belonged to her. Now she had this near-stranger man. That is till help came, of course. He was her own, and she was not alone.

She brought the animals out of the helicopter, opened a tin of meat and fed them. She gave them the tiniest reasonable amount of water because she supposed it might be quite a time before they were found. It was blistering hot now, but when the temperature fell in the night it would be bitterly cold. The book of instructions with the calamity kit said to spread a plastic sheet on the ground so that condensation would gather a few thimblefuls of water.

'I don't have a thimble to measure,' she said, still talking to herself. It was the only way to pass time. Not to worry. She needed all her wits and had to stay calm. Any minute now she might be afraid or she might start talking to the ants, even the bardies gnawing their way in the branch axles of the trees.

'If we run low on food,' she told the animals, 'I can start feeding you on the bardies. They're only worms but I know the aborigines eat them. So no complaints from you.'

Mentioning aborigines reminded her of something. Jard had said he'd drop down by Mister Falldown's camp to deliver the pup early. It was past mid-afternoon now. Mister Falldown trusted Jard. He would know Jard would keep his word. So he would know something had gone wrong when Jard didn't arrive on time.

Who else would know?

Mardie was unsure about that. At the Dig-in they would think maybe Jard had gone back to the out-camp. He was known to be a 'loner'. He operated as a 'loner' . . . for reasons still unknown to Mardie. And which reasons didn't matter any more for now.

At The Breakaway there had been suggestions she might be invited to the Mansell homestead. The Richies could think she was there and might not contact Mansell till the Session on the transceiver. After sun-down. Then it would be too late to find anyone at all before morning. Night was very dark in the outback when there was no moonlight. And it was new-moon time, so there wouldn't be any light to speak of. Except for the stars. They were very bright – the stars in the outback.

And there would be Mister Falldown.

Mardie went to the 'copter and brought out the one and

only bush rug and the one sheet of plastic she could find. When the heat went out of the land she would put the rug over Jard, and spread out the plastic sheet, pinned down by stones to catch those thimbles of water. Just in case . . .

All the time these activities – and Mardie's think-talk processes – were going on, she had kept at intervals feeding little drops of water into Jard's mouth. She mustn't allow him to dehydrate. She knew that much though where she had learned it she did not know.

At the back of her mind she thought about 'shock' too. Where had she heard or learned that you treated patients suffering from shock by keeping them warm? 'Warmth is imperative!'

Those occasional rigors Jard kept having must be something to do with shock.

'Well, not to worry,' she told Dingo Pup. 'The heat is still on the land so the Boss is warm enough right now. I'll maybe have to double the rug over him come night. Maybe I'd just better massage his limbs more often. Just in case it does some good. I don't really know . . .'

Somehow admitting this to herself, let alone to the wild dog, was suddenly the last straw. She was sitting on the ground beside Jard and she bent over, put her head on her knees and cried. Her mind had been behaving stupidly, like a child's. But then she'd been hit on the head too. She thought probably she was a little out of her mind. Do minds hurt the same way as bodies hurt? Because her body hurt everywhere, anyway.

'It's a pity tears are salt,' she said ten minutes later – this time to Digger. 'Otherwise we could use them for water some time next week if we run short.'

She was, of course, not admitting they'd still be here, lost, one week hence. She wasn't admitting anything except her very real pain. Her limbs seemed to keep on paining and aching. She would like very much to have a little lie down and go to sleep. She couldn't afford to do this, of course. She had to look after . . . after . . .

But she did.

Suddenly without volition she slowly rolled over on the ground beside Jard. And fell instantly into a stupor kind of sleep. She was utterly, completely finished. A state beyond her control.

The sun went down and Dingo Pup howled. This was because

night was his natural talking time. Digger had crept over and curled himself up in the hollow of Mardie's back. He was laying claims for a warm spot against the cold of the night. And it was the cold that woke Mardie. Some time in her half-sleep she had tucked the bush rug in tight around Jard.

Now she reached for the can standing by the tree trunk and dripped more water in Jard's mouth. She wished she had tried to use that smashed up two-way speaker in the helicopter again. Yet she knew in her heart it had been broken beyond repair.

She was dressed only in cotton clothes and the cold was beginning to chill her skin. She opened another small tin of meat and shared it with Digger and Dingo Pup.

'And you shut up!' she cautioned Dingo Pup. 'Any howling from you in the night and I'll up and wallop you, even though I am getting a bit soft-hearted about you. It's not much fun for you, tied in that sugar bag, all except for your head sticking out. But it's not much fun for the rest of us either. I'm a lot colder than you are. I've nothing to wrap round me. You've got that bag.'

She lay down beside Jard again, curling into his body as Digger curled into hers. She remembered reading somewhere, before she'd ever come up north, that the *ground* temperature at night could drop as low as nineteen degrees in the inland at this time of the year.

Jard wouldn't mind her curling into him, tight, sharing a little bit of the rug with him – because he wouldn't ever know, would he?

It was cold. Then, much later, it was colder and colder and colder.

She was shivering herself but every now and again Jard's rigors were stronger than they had been in the day time. And it had been *hot* then. These rigors must be shock symptoms getting worse. She crawled right in under the rug with him and put her arms round him. She held him tight to her so he might get the warmth from her body.

A little rivulet of tears ran down her cheeks. He was *here*. Yet he was a stranger. Here in this moment of time she had to care for him. Keep him warm. Save him.

In the small hours of the morning it became yet colder still. Jard was shivering all the time now.

Mardie took one moment to think, then stopped thinking because she knew that thinking of what she was about to do would frighten her into a cold grave – with or without Jard, Digger and Dingo Pup.

She took off Jard's shirt. Stripped herself of all her clothes except her panties, and drew Digger in under Jard's feet to add his warmth. Then gently, almost lovingly because he was injured and she was caring for him the only way she knew possible, she curled herself, skin to skin, around him. She could do better. She would provide him with the greatest warmth possible. The human warmth of *two bodies*, and not even the warmth of her breath wasted.

She turned him over on his near side so his body, against her body, lay in her arms. His face and head lay in the curve of her neck and she clasped him tightly to herself. Nothing between them. But caring.

She did not think of anything except: This is the only way – my warmth for him.

Exhaustion came to Mardie's aid at long last. She fell asleep.

Mardie did not know what aroused her in the false dawn before morning. It was not the real dawn but only that grey light that preceded it, which would later give way to the heralding flags of the rising sun.

Then she realized what had woken her. It was the sound of crushing sticks and bush leafery under boots.

She lifted her head.

They were standing a few yards away. Two bush-whacker types. Beardy and rough-dressed. They stared down at the girl and man lying cradled together under the rug.

'Hell's bells – it's Hunter,' said one. 'Who'd have bloody-all thought it. Grounded with a dame!'

Because of the light they would not have seen the wrecked 'copter in the trees a hundred yards away.

The pains and aches of yesterday were agony today, Mardie realized. She could have cried out as she sat up. Help at last. That was all she thought.

The aches made her awkward, clumsy. She fumbled the rug and it fell off.

'For crying out loud!' the first man said again.

'Help . . . *please*. We're hurt . . .' Mardie began.

The second man laughed, disbelieving.

Mardie realized they could not see the fallen helicopter.

She tried to explain.

'We had an accident. A crash . . .' she began, almost piteously, hardly aware of anything but the searing pain down her back.

'We need help . . .' she began weakly.

The first man was staring at Jard Hunter. Mardie saw that they both carried rifles. They were probably hunters . . . dingo-shooters . . . or something. The first man looked startled and he jerked the butt of his gun into his mate's ribs.

'Out of here, mate,' he said. 'Smart. Hunter'll recognize us.'

The second man switched his stare from Mardie to Jard.

'You said it, boy,' he almost snarled. Or did Mardie dream it?

They turned and went off fast through the bush with boot treads like the thundering of herds.

'Please!' Mardie called. '*Please . . . please wait . . .*'

She threw the rug aside and tried as she half rose to drag her clothes up from somewhere round her feet.

The men were going, and going fast.

'Please get help! Please get help!' she called. She tried to get to her feet.

Yesterday's bruises had set. Her rattled bones were stiff. She only got half up, then slumped and fell back. As she did so her face was turned to Jard again, but her eyes were closed. She was dazed by her own minor agonies. And the pity of it because they had gone. She had not been able to stop them.

They had not stayed to help. There was a reason somewhere. Something to do with Jard.

Her lids flew open and looked straight into his eyes. He was looking at her . . . right into her face . . . his own not six inches away.

Then slowly – as if desperately tired – his lids dropped and his eyes closed again.

Mardie put her cheek against his. 'I'm so sorry,' she said, tears in her eyes. 'So very sorry. I . . . I didn't stop them. I tried . . .'

She could not get up quickly enough and run after them. That was not only the stiffness in her whole body, but because she was all but naked. And Jard was that way too!

She had not wanted him ever to know. For one half-light

moment he had been conscious. Would he remember?

She didn't know. So she gave in and cried on to his shoulder. It was all too much! She'd done her best. But they had gone away. *Just gone!* She couldn't really quite believe it.

The false dawn became the real dawn and the sun was gold and striped fan-wise against a pale pale blue sky. There was a tossing of tree leaves in the early morning wind. This was the wind that always blew from the east across the desert in the morning. It was also cold. But it did not have the fierce bite in it that the cold of bottom temperatures in the midnight and early hours of morning had. In three hours' time that land breeze would have dropped and God's Wrath would fall on the land again, with the blistering heat of hell in it.

Mardie wiped the back of her hand across her eyes and looked at Jard again. But his eyes were closed – sort-of slightly as if the lids wanted to flicker but couldn't quite make it.

She sat up, pulled the rug right over them again, and began to pull on her clothes.

Then she heard yet another sound in the bush.

Not the thrashing of heavy boots this time. A soft sound, yet a steady one as of someone coming purposefully but with a natural quietness.

She looked through the trees and blinked her eyes to see the better. The shadow coming through the bush was dark. Old clothes. An old shabby broad-brimmed hat. A dark face.

Mardie felt as if it was not the sun that had risen but the whole of heaven that had opened up with glory. A bush angel had come.

'*Mister Falldown!*'

She said it softly because of the lump in her throat.

After that everything was all right.

Mister Falldown made the kind of bush fire that wouldn't spread and make a holocaust of the whole area. A fire was that dangerous thing the wind could carry many many miles. Mardie hadn't been able to make a fire last night because she hadn't had the strength to lever the spade under the sand and through the gravel to clear a safety break. The ground had been rock hard and the low bushes dry and wire-tough. Her own arms and back had been too stiff with pain – even if they'd had the muscular strength. She had not dared a fire because she knew of that prevailing morning wind. It even reached The Breakaway each morning with the scent of distant border lands, not one, but *two* deserts away.

Jard opened his eyes again. Mister Falldown nodded.

'Him come-along all right,' he said. 'Bime-bye maybe. You watch him, Missy. I'll send up this smoke signal – *so*! Airplane come over maybe soon. Police Land-Rover come bime-bye. You watch 'em. Okay?'

Mardie sat, arms wrapped round her knees and watched while Mister Falldown did all the things a bushman knew how to do.

He made a fire in a wide circle of sand, and damped it down with the greener leaves of low trees. He ripped out a floor mat from the 'copter, then proceeded to cover and uncover the gathering flames and smoke of his carefully controlled fire. Sometimes he let a long thin spiral of smoke streak up beam-on straight for heaven. Sometimes he manipulated the mat off and on over the fire so that round clouds of smoke, like grey cotton-wool balls, floated slowly and gracefully upwards. quietly to disperse away westwards as the land breeze carried them off.

Next he took two of the tins of canned meat and rolled the contents between the palms of his hands into small balls. He put these in the hot sand under the fire coals for a few minutes. When heated, and smelling like heaven, he set them out in a row on a stone. When they were cool he gave some to Mardie. Then he fed Jard, crumb by crumb, watching carefully to see that each crumb was swallowed, and that he did not choke on one. He fed and watered the dogs.

Time passed.

This feeding of the patient had taken a long time because the barely conscious Jard could swallow only the tiniest morsel. In between several such morsels Mister Falldown dripped the water down his throat. The old bushman watched carefully to see that after each dose of meat crumbs or water Jard moved the muscles of his throat. Now and again Mister Falldown massaged the muscles himself with his broad, flat, dark hands.

'He'll do okay, this feller,' he said. In all this time he hadn't uttered more than half a dozen sentences.

Mardie had given herself up to being a patient now. Deep in her being – without knowing or having enough mental strength to think it all out – she knew her task was over.

It didn't matter any more that the two men who had come just before dawn had gone off leaving them helpless. She would think about them later. Perhaps another day.

Funny, but it was an effort even to think at all. It didn't matter any more. The old man out of the bush – with the forgotten memory – had come. He was God in another guise. All would be well. Now she could lie down and have another little sleep. This, because her head was dizzy again.

The plane came about mid-morning. The smoke signals had sent their message. It had had to land some long distance away where the strip of bushland ended and the stony desert could provide a landing ground. Not one, but two Land-Rovers came later. One she could recognize as the police vehicle by its centre roof radio mast and the blue-red flashing light.

Mardie couldn't focus her attention any more. There seemed a lot of people about. Mostly there was Joanna, so the other Land-Rover must have come from the Dig-in. The plane was from the Royal Flying Doctor Service. She heard someone saying that.

Joanna seemed to stop being a geologist and had become a nurse. The way she stripped off Jard and helped the pilot from the Flying Doctor Service! Her directness and efficiency were marvels to watch. For one terrifying crash and one long night he had belonged to Mardie. Now he was Joanna's. Mardie wondered why she minded. When Joanna had attended to Jard she came over to Mardie and went to work with fingers like steel rods, feeling here, poking there. Oh yes. She was very efficient. All the time as she worked the pilot was two-waying the information Joanna gave him back to the doctor at Base.

Mardie felt sad. Oh, to be Joanna! Joanna would have managed through the night so much better. She wouldn't have fallen asleep. She would not have kept getting dizzy. Mardie was sure of this. Joanna was the sort of person born to survive – *the right way.* That would be to keep her head all the time. There probably wouldn't even have been a crash if Joanna had been there instead of Mardie, the girl from a town. She would have been on the look-out, and have seen the eagles in time.

'There you are,' Joanna said, kindly now. She had finished pushing, pulling and poking Mardie. 'You'll be all right. Nothing broken. No internal swelling so no haemorrhage, I think. Dr Fells at Base seems to be satisfied. He'll keep in touch.' She finished pulling Mardie's clothes on again, while Mardie herself wondered why she didn't tell Joanna about the two early morning bushmen who had run off and deserted them.

She doesn't have to know everything that happened, she thought. I couldn't ever tell her about lying all night without clothes, to keep Jard warm. I couldn't ever tell anyone that. They wouldn't understand . . .

Mister Falldown was standing looking down at her. She had a feeling Mister Falldown *knew*. About the no-clothes too. *She knew that he knew – she had done the right thing.* His dark eyes said so.

'Mister Falldown . . .?'

'You be okay, Missy. You did good thing all right,' was all he said.

'Thank you, Mister Falldown.' She said this from her heart.

EIGHT

'Davy!' Joanna called. 'I think you'd better take Mardie in the Land-Rover. Dr Fells at Base says he'll drop down at The Breakaway and give her a detailed run-over after he's seen Jard at the Regional Hospital. Will you take Mister and those two animals along with you?'

'Sure, sure!'

That was a sound Mardie knew. She turned her head. The several men who had come in the Land-Rovers had been standing politely away while Joanna had been giving Mardie the run-over. One or two of them had been looking over the damaged 'copter. Now someone was standing looking down at her. He had a gorgeous smile. She knew he had to be David Ashton from the Dig-in.

'Hallo! How's the Voice?' he asked, and his smile grew better still.

'David! I knew it was you – the way you said "Sure, sure".'

'None other. We meet in strange places, don't we?'

He bent down and dropped a kiss on her forehead. 'Good girl, Mardie,' he said. 'You did a wonderful job. How in the name of fortune did you get Jard out of that 'copter?'

'I don't know. I pushed and pulled. And he just came – sort-of.'

'Like a lamb to the fold?' David's grin was mischievous.

He knows – he guesses, she thought. But how could he?

They were lifting Jard on a litter. Joanna was walking beside it, holding his hand.

'I'm coming with you,' Joanna said to the pilot, meaning it.

'I'd take her,' David advised him. 'She'll be the best right hand you've ever had. She always has her own way anyhow.'

'So I've heard,' the pilot grinned. 'Not always my luck to have a good-looking girl to hold a patient's hand.' He turned to Mardie.

'Dr Fells will be seeing you, Mardie,' he said. 'Keep moving when you get home. Restricted activity only, but it will keep those muscles from stiffening.'

He turned away, bringing up the rear of the little procession, now disappearing through the bush into and beyond the tree belt.

Mardie watched them go.

She was suddenly aware of David's eyes on her.

'Sad to see them go now it's all over?' he asked. 'Not to worry, Mardie. He's in good hands. Joanna's the best ever at rendering First Aid. The pilot may need that. They'll have to keep the plane at five hundred feet. Not above. It's not pressurized and they can't risk a patient's reactions at height.'

'You think . . .?'

'Stunned at first and maybe slight concussion. How slight will be checked at the hospital. Meantime they have to fly the plane low – just as a precaution.'

'Could that be dangerous? How high are the mesas?'

'He'll fly round them.'

'But there may be more eagles – '

'Eagles don't usually rush aeroplanes. It's mostly the 'copters that attract them. Our 'copters don't fly high. They're lower and slower. The blades whirling horizontally fascinate them.'

'Like cars to kangaroos?'

'Exactly. The cars don't so often hit the kangaroos. The 'roos hit the cars. Mostly because they're attracted to the moving objects. And to moving lights at night.'

Mardie nodded.

Her eyes were following the progress of the rescue party,

now disappearing through the trees.

David was still watching her. She shook her head, brushing some thought away that no longer had any relevance to this little group left behind.

'Can we take Mister Falldown with us, David?'

'Mister has gone, Mardie,' David said gently.

'Gone? Oh no! But how?'

'Silently. Like the shades of night. You don't hear him come and you don't hear him go. That's Mister Falldown's way. Incidentally he's taken that flaming dingo pup with him.'

'Don't call the pup a flaming anything, David,' Mardie said, bristling. 'He was here . . . with us. And Digger too. And Jard. He . . .'

'Belonged to the experience? That killer pup belongs to Mister, Mardie, and Mister's taken his possession and gone. That's all there is to it. We'll take Digger with us.'

'But he must have walked miles and miles and miles to get here.'

'And he'll walk miles and miles back. Then forget to remember it happened. Let it be, sweetheart. It's his way of life and his way of doing things.'

'Not like the two men who came when it was barely daylight. They recognized Jard. Then they just went for their lives. They didn't want to help us.'

'*Two men*? Out in this stretch of country?' David asked sharply. 'What were they like? No, wait! We'll get you aboard the Land-Rover first. Then tell me about them later. It's important, Mardie, so be a lamb and spend the trip home remembering every detail. Jard's not the only person who'll want to know about that pair. *No one* deserts a stranded person in the outback. Unless, of course, they're on the run themselves!'

'Well, before I forget one thing. They had guns. Or rifles. I don't know the difference. Do dingo-shooters use rifles or guns?'

'If they were dingo-shooters, they'd have carried rifles, Mardie, but they *wouldn't* have cleared out. Not on your life. Don't ask any more questions, like a good girl. Just keep your efforts for remembering. Right?'

Mardie nodded. It was easier to be docile than not. Her brain had stopped whizzing at irregular intervals but it still had that vaguely depleted feeling.

It would be wonderful to go to bed for a week, she thought. Except that she didn't want to be a dead weight on the Richies.

No. She would have to get on with that will-power business again. It had worked – getting Jard out of that 'copter. That is, if will-power was the same thing as God.

Mardie was so wrapped up in these speculative thoughts that she hardly noticed how painful it was to walk, even with help, to the Land-Rover. She did have one reflective moment when she thought that perhaps David, God and will power *all* had something in common. David's strong arm took most of her weight and his hands were so gentle she wanted to thank him, but didn't quite know how. Her voice had gone all unsteady again.

But she was *not going to cry*!

Oh well! Tomorrow would be another day. Besides she had a little ordering around to do herself then. Those workmen hadn't made a true line along the cement foundations for her motel units.

Willy nilly, tomorrow she had things to do – about *them*.

The Land-Rover was not exactly the most comfortable vehicle as it thundered its way across trackless bush back towards the gravel plain. Mardie did not complain. She was so thankful to be saved. Besides the Rover could go anywhere – even uncomfortably – because it had a four-wheel drive. A comforting thought that.

'Any good at guessing games, Mardie?' David was wearing his best-friend two-way radio voice.

'If they're easy ones,' she admitted meekly.

'Okay. What's the answer to this one? We're using front-wheel drive at the moment. What shall we do if it breaks down?'

'Get out and mend it. That is, if you know how –'

'No, love. Just change over to rear-wheel drive.' His laugh was music to Mardie's ears.

The guessing game went on, while David and the two men kept her amused. Some of their outback yarns would have made her grandmother's hair stand on end, but Mardie didn't care. They were bright company for a girl still racked with one pain here and two pains there every time the Rover lurched over a bad surface. But each time it did that David made a new joke, or asked a funny riddle.

But it was Joanna who was to hold Jard's hand on the litter! And on the plane too. It was Joanna who was the saviour now!

As they neared The Breakaway some hours later, Mardie had almost forgotten that pain mattered so very much. It was something one came to live with. It wasn't too bad – once one was thinking of something else.

They were kind, these three men, and they laughed a lot. Nearly all the time, in fact.

That wonderful music of the world – laughter! This time it was the healer too.

Mardie had always thought it was a wonderful thing to see stars on a moonless night, or a sunset that blazed across a windless sky on a heat-wave sun-down. Now she decided the most wonderful thing of all was the sound of laughter. The panacea – even for envy!

It meant you were one of a group. You belonged. She would never feel really alone again. She was sure of that. She had a 're-born' feeling since she'd come out to the out-back. Never again to be the 'third one out' as at home.

When the Land-Rover pulled in at The Breakaway there were Mr and Mrs Richie running out to meet them!

'Oh, Mardie darling, are you all right?' Mrs Richie had tears in her eyes.

'Mardie girl! You're safe? Nothing broken?' Mr Richie was in a proper flap. The way he advanced on her made Mardie temporarily scared that she might have, once again, to go through that prodding, pushing, bending and stretching she had already suffered at Joanna's not-so-gentle hands. But Mr Richie had only come to take her cheeks between his hands and kiss her.

'She's as right as rain!' David answered for her. He slammed tight the brakes and opened the drive door. 'The pertest girl east of the black stump, Mrs R. Full of cheek. How's the kettle? On the boil?'

'Yes, and there's a bottle of champagne out on the bar counter waiting for you men.'

Everyone was giving a hand to help Mardie dismount from the Land-Rover.

'In a bucket of ice?' David demanded over Mardie's head.

'Yes, and another ice bucket in the freezer waiting for a hammer to crack it up.'

David threw a look over his shoulder.

'Pete? For Pete's sake, get a hammer out of the tool box. We're about to need it. Mardie girl, keep still. I'm going to carry you over the doorstep with or without your consent. I mightn't be the bridegroom yet but I'm about to get me some practice.'

So they laughed. All of them. Mrs Richie laughed through her near-tears, as in a triumphal procession they carried Mardie into The Breakaway's best room, then on to the sofa.

It might have been a grand party as if to celebrate her return from a moon walk.

Yet there was something more behind their quips and their deliberate laughter.

Thought of Jard? Yes, that was there, only part hidden.

He was in good hands and everyone knew that. Yet there was something else. Over their glasses came a quick exchange of glances between David and Pete, then sort-of casually Pete disappeared. He came back ten minutes later and exchanged nods with David.

More than once Mrs Richie whispered in the corner to her husband. *Something*, Mardie thought, *is going on*.

'I'm lying here on this sofa and I don't know whether it means I'm Queen of the May, or a serious patient,' she said. 'Would you all please be kind enough to tell me what's the mystery in the air?'

'Mystery?' They looked aghast as if she had suggested something outrageous.

'Well, I'll ask the questions that puzzle *me*,' she said. 'Joanna's gone with the Flying Doctor's pilot. How and when will she get back? We all want to know how well or bad Jard might be. Question two. What has happened to Mr Falldown? And how did he *know* where we were and that something serious had happened? Question three is only about the ute, and how will we get it back from Mansell's paddock?'

'Question three is the easiest answered,' David said with a grin. 'If the Vet could land his plane at Mansell's corner paddock, so could the Flying Doctor. He will drop Joanna off there and *she'll* bring your ute back. Authority for any information? The Richies and the "session" over the transceiver.'

'Then why the whispering?'

'Well, Mardie darling,' Mr Richie said, 'like the good girl you are, you locked the ute and took the car keys with you.'

'And Pete went outside,' David went on, 'to get on to *our*

two-way code to tell Jo how to pick the lock. Couldn't put that over the public Session, you know. All the baddies listening in would be taking a lesson on how to pick car locks.'

They all laughed and again Mr Richie filled the men's glasses. Mrs Richie brought Mardie a glass of milk.

'Have to play safe with that, dear,' she said. 'If milk can't harm a kitten, it won't hurt you.'

'How clever can Joanna be!' Mardie said, shaking her head thoughtfully. 'I wish I had her brains. A geologist, a cook, a beauty expert, a nurse and now a lock-picker.'

'I'd rather take her good looks – *as one of my portable possessions of course*,' the youngest of the trio, Alan Barnes, said.

'I'll drink to that.' Pete raised his glass in a meaningful way.

Mardie wished she had all Joanna's brains and her everything else. But then who wouldn't? Since Joanna used them all with the maximum efficiency and maximum effect – then good luck to her! Obviously the right person was rightly gifted and that's the way it was.

Not to be envious though! She, *Mardie*, had had her own gift from the gods. She had held this injured man in her arms all night, body to body, to keep him warm and perhaps – who knows? – saved him from death from shock and because of the cold. To have done that one thing once meant she had done *something* that mattered.

In the morning, just for one moment he had opened his eyes. She had seen that the pupils of his eyes were evenly matched, and she was sure – from schoolgirl days when she had been hit on the head with a hockey ball – that the even matching of the eye pupils had been most important evidence. It had meant that she had suffered from nothing more than a nasty crack. No severe haemorrhage. No brain damage. And so, thank God, with Jard.

They were all standing looking at her.

'You're too quiet, Mardie. What's worrying you?' David asked.

'Why, nothing. I was thinking of something that happened to me once when I was at school. Do you think Jard was knocked unconscious and that there is nothing more serious than that?'

'Fairly certain of it. There's bound to be some after-effects of shock, of course. That's usually one nasty aspect of a crash. They'll treat him for that as a top priority at the hospital. The doctor will fix all that. It's his business. But what does that have to do with you being at school? You can read and write, can't you, sweetheart?'

'I like you calling me "sweetheart", David. It sounds friendly. Yes, I can read and write. And manage algebra now and again. What I'm trying to add up is something in my *second* question. How did Mister Falldown know what had happened? And *where* to look for us?'

'It's Wednesday, Mardie,' Mrs Richie reminded her. 'So yesterday was Tuesday – the day Mister Falldown should have come in for his stores. When the police came over on the blower as they usually do, we had to tell them he hadn't come in. They went out to his camp and, as is routine, took their tracker with them.'

'Old Mister hasn't forgotten all he pretends he's forgotten,' Mr Richie interrupted with a chuckle. 'He knew darn-all a tracker would come. And he remembered to leave the kind of tracks the tracker would understand and read. In other words, *his* kind of message.'

'Quite a one is our Mister Falldown – when he's up to something,' Pete said with a laugh.

'But how on earth did he know *where* to look? In which direction?'

'Old Mister is a bushman and he knows everything that happens in his stretch of country,' David said. 'He knows that mesa range out there has a strong water seepage. He wouldn't understand the geological terms for a "water catchment", but he knows there's underground water running along the base line of those mesas. He was the first to take Jard out there. What's more, he knows Jard can't keep from taking a look at the place every time he takes the 'copter for a ride.'

Mardie made a little move.

'He didn't go just to take *me* for a pleasure trip? It wasn't because of my bright eyes?' She hoped they didn't see her disappointment. She had to make a joke of it, of course. 'He wanted to go and look at his beloved water tracks, so he took a bird along just for the company! Then the other birds got him. I mean the big feathered ones.'

They all laughed again.

'That's just about it.' David's eyes were twinkling.

'This time it was a couple of wedge-tails that had him.

Not a mini skirt. He'll get plenty of chipping about that – don't you fret!'

'Oh dear!' Mrs Richie said, ruffled. 'We shouldn't be making fun about him. After all, he is ill in hospital.'

'He has Joanna to hold his hand,' Pete said consolingly.

'Till she brings the ute back,' Mr Richie added drily. 'Well, the sooner it's all over, the better. Meantime we have Mister Falldown to thank for being a godsend of a bushman.'

'Don't forget the police with their two-way, and the Dig-in with theirs,' David added. 'After all – we were there too!'

Yes, but not all night, Mardie thought. Not cold and close together – with my arms round him.

The Breakaway was a busy place for days. Apart from the workmen and the first bricks rising above the cement foundations for the motel units, there came the usual through-travellers stopping for petrol, a drink, stores and a chat.

Then two days later Joanna came with Mardie's ute.

'Why I bothered, I'll never know!' she said. 'After all, Mansell could have sent their jackeroo over with the wretched thing. It really is a clanger, Mardie. Time The Breakaway bought a new one.'

Mardie, still under orders to take it easy, thought about this too. She passed over the bit about the ute being a clanger.

'Perhaps, out there at Mansell, they didn't want their jackeroo to learn how to pick car locks,' she said with a laugh. She was glad to see Joanna. It was company to have someone her own age, but she wished she could get past her feeling of being over-awed by all the things Joanna could do. Then there was the little matter of her own wishful thinking because Joanna was, as usual, wonderful to look at. Even in the emergency of rushing out to the rescue from the Dig-in she hadn't forgotten her make-up case. Nor her brush and comb. And a change of clothes.

Joanna explained these last away airily. 'After all, when you're around a crash-up in the outback you don't know how long you might be stuck there nursing the injured.'

'You are always prepared? They happen that often?'

'A couple of weeks before you came up a truck turned over on the creek bridge between Mansell and Mytana Station. The driver was killed so there was no staying around then. Five weeks before that the same thing happened, and that time we did have to stay around. The driver and his mate were alive all right, but the creek was flooded, so the Flying Doctor Service was grounded. The stations couldn't even get a Land-Rover over to this side of the river. There was quite a bit of swabbing and bandaging to get on with then!'

Mardie's eyes widened in a real admiration of Joanna's many abilities.

'How did you learn all these wonder things?' she asked. 'I mean bandaging, and all that?'

'When I decided I wanted to be a field geologist, not a desk-bound chartist, *I used my brains*. Good advice that, Mardie! Always use your brains first, not later. I took a First Aid Ambulance course. I went to the Land-Rover firm and took a routine course in the mechanics of the thing. By the way that's a *Regulation Must* for Government geologists. Not that they use any women in the field.'

'Anything more?' Mardie asked, still wide-eyed.

'Yes. I took a beauty care course as a package deal. Face lotions, oil, moisturizer, lipstick, the lot. I did *not* intend to get frazzled out by the heat.'

Mardie was still blinking.

'So?' Joanna asked.

'I'm amazed! How thorough can anyone be!'

'Meaning me? Well, that's the way I set out to be. I'm that way about my possessions too, including men friends. So come clean, Mardie. How come Jard made a mistake about those wedge-tails? He wasn't looking in the wrong direction, by any chance? Gazing into other eyes, or some such?'

Mardie was puzzled. She hadn't quite caught Joanna's meaning.

'I guess one's looking round about all the time, when flying a 'copter. It's not the same as flying a plane, is it? He certainly wasn't heading to land in that bush strip. He wasn't heading to land anywhere. He just *fell*. Like a meteorite; bang out of the sky. We were flying fairly low, thank goodness.'

Joanna stretched her arms above her head as if about to yawn. 'Oh well!' she said. 'I guess he'll tell us all about it when he's well enough.'

'Does he remember *everything* about it?' Mardie asked cautiously. She pretended to be interested in the state of her hands.

'He says so. But doesn't go into details, *yet*. After all, he is still getting over a nasty bash on the head. One thing for certain . . . he was very pleased to see me sitting there when he did wake up. I never saw a sweeter grin in my life. However, he didn't remember how he got there.'

Joanna stood up and walked to the window. 'You won't mind if I don't tell you his exact words, will you?' she said. 'They were very private.'

'No, of course I don't mind.' Mardie's small laugh somehow was mixed up with her cheek muscles and this felt rather painful. 'You are old friends. And good friends.'

Joanna turned round. 'More than that,' she said succinctly. 'But we'll talk about that another day. Meantime David Ashton is crazy for you to come out to the Dig-in. By earth-bound passage this time. Gravel track only. You will come, won't you? We're probably bringing the big diamond drill in shortly. Depends on the Company's directors. Testing the depth of the intersections at strike length, you know. That will be in the next week or two if it can be arranged. I doubt if Jard will be out there at the time but you'll have had more than enough of his company I guess. After all, he did rather let you down.'

'He didn't let me down. We *fell* down,' Mardie insisted. 'The 'copter just *fell*. Jard didn't have anything to do with it. Except he was there. Same as I was there. One eagle came through the wind-screen and the other must have got mixed up with the top works. The blades went askew and came clean off. You must have *seen* the broken wind-screen and the – '

'Hush, Mardie,' Joanna said, using kindly tones this time. Talking to a child. 'You really must stop thinking about it. And keeping on about this "fell down" thing. It's bad for you to dwell on it after such a traumatic experience . . .'

'I know you're a very good nurse, Joanna. You're in charge of the First Aid room out there at Dig-in, aren't you? What with all that First Aid training – not to mention the beauty care, and being a scientist. But, *please*. What is a traumatic experience?'

'To put it simply, it's an experience that leaves an after-math of strain and anxiety. a desire to *churn* things over and over. Keep repeating oneself. Letting it get one *down*!'

'And now you've put it into simple English for me!'

Joanna laughed. 'Mardie, dear, you really are quite a pet, but you mustn't take things so seriously. You must try to forget the whole experience. This is important because there *can* be after-effects.'

It was Mardie's turn to stare through the window. She wasn't sure that Joanna wasn't wishing simple-mindedness and traumatic aftermaths on her by way of suggestion. But, in that case, someone with a scientific training, a First Aid training, and a beauty care training would know what she was doing. Or wouldn't she?

'I'll tell you what I do take seriously,' she said at last. 'It's when those men out there don't put a spirit level along the brick-line as they lay the brick, and don't drop a plumb-line down the doorway gaps so the doors will really fit. That is when they come. Funny how some types . . . you know, skilled *trained people* . . . sometimes need *watching*.' She glanced at Joanna with one eyebrow just the smallest bit lifted. This time the other girl had missed the message. Actually, for the fraction of a second Mardie thought she herself was the meanie, and was rather glad Joanna had not clicked.

NINE

Other visitors came and went.

The Flying Doctor dropped down on the landing ground east side of the bitumen. He examined Mardie and pronounced her fit enough to take on a marathon walkathon any time she felt like it. He stayed for lunch and told amusing stories about people who thought they were ill in the remote vastnesses of the outback when all that was wrong was that they were newcomers, and weren't used to eating kangaroo steak in large quantities. Or that a master bull-ant wasn't a scorpion and, if bitten, they wouldn't die in spite of a large gland popping up under the arm.

One of the workmen on Mardie's new building had a mildly poisoned finger and Dr Fells treated that. He took the plastic bindings off Digger's leg, and pronounced a lump in Mr Richie's wrist as a boil and not a growth – a fear Mr Richie had been secretly nursing for four days.

'Any more queries, complaints or imaginary pains?' he asked with a grin as he glanced round the assembled group which consisted of The Breakaway's household, builders, and a host of young aborigines who, like the early morning shades cast by the mulgas against the morning sunrise sky, had crept in from unimaginable distances. They had come to see the Magic Flying Man who was here to cure all ills and who cast goodwill about as vagrantly as he might crumbs to colourful birds.

There was a general shaking of heads as he was escorted by this motley posse back across the bitumen and over the landing ground to the aeroplane which had the enchanting and magic letters printed on its sides: *Royal Flying Doctor Service.* God's greatest gift to the outback.

The next drop-ins were the strangest of all. Two of them; and Mardie had seen them before. But two weeks before this visitation, David Ashton came through on the two-way from the Dig-in.

'How's Bickleys Brandy this morning? It's your sweetheart from Red Wine calling.'

'As if I wouldn't know your voice.' There was a smile in Mardie's voice. 'I've been dying to hear from you, David. Each time I've called Red Wine you've been out at the drill site. There's always been someone else on call.'

'What do you specially want to know, love? The only messages we've had were all about stores.'

'How Jard is getting on, of course. After all, I have a vested interest. We fell down out of that sky together. Remember?'

'That's what I'm calling you about. I'll have to take second interest for the next five minutes, won't I? So count your words. Here comes someone.'

Mardie drew in a deep breath. Could it be . . .?

Jard's voice came over the air. Quiet, sort-of contained, yet with that soft but certain note in it.

'Hallo, Mardie. Jard Hunter calling. How are you?'

It seemed so formal. Yet there was a certain something in it that made Mardie's heart turn. There was a lump in her throat but she tried not to let its presence come through.

'Fine,' she said, mustering brightness like gold dust out of the air. 'Never better in my life. Bruises gone, aches vanished. But what about you? I knew you were all right. I heard it over the session. But I didn't know how much all right.'

'I'd have called you over the Session, Mardie, to say "thank you". But in this case it would sound too personal to have the whole world listening in.'

'You don't have to say thank you for anything, Jard. It was nothing. Nothing at all. I want to know *how you are.*

Any permanent . . . well, scars . . . or such things?'

'A stiff leg – temporary only. One bent little finger – you'd hardly notice. A fine line where they put a row of stitches in my head – quite unnecessarily. But you know what doctors are. Give them a skin cut and they hassle for a needle. I'm sorry I can't come over to thank you personally just yet. I would have done so when they first brought me back to the Dig-in, but I can't drive until my leg loosens up a bit. The damn thing won't operate the accelerator pedal *yet.*'

'Oh . . . I am sorry. About your leg, of course. And about your not coming over too. I would like to see you.'

'Yes. We have to get together with the Law, I'm afraid. They need a record of what happened, and meantime the Company is sending up an insurance expert about the 'copter. They'll both need your evidence. Do you remember exactly what happened?'

'Only at first – when the blades made that dreadful clanging noise on the roof. I hope I'll be able to help, Jard, but it all happened so quickly. I was busy saving myself and not thinking about how and what was actually happening . . . I mean, second by second. It was all so quick. That eagle came beak-first straight through the windscreen at your head. I do remember that.'

There was a silence.

'Over to you, Jard,' Mardie said, in case he hadn't flicked the switch and was still waiting for her to go on speaking.

'Yes. I'm on air, Mardie. Sorry to take so long about it. Is this a good time to ask you how on earth you got me out of that cockpit?'

'Well . . . I was doing things . . . so I wasn't *thinking.* I can't remember all the details – *quite.* Couldn't we leave it awhile? And Jard? You haven't lost your memory or anything like that, have you?' An almost hopeful note crept into her voice. She wanted to beg him *not* to remember the *night.* 'I mean – sometimes it happens about forgetting what has happened after an accident.'

'Some of it, Mardie. Things are blank after I cracked my head on the panel, of course. But not in any other way. I'm not Mister Falldown-the-Second, if that is what you're thinking. I haven't forgotten who I am, or where from.'

There was such a long pause that Jard said, 'Over to you still, Mardie. I haven't switched across.'

The lump that had been in Mardie's throat had disappeared but there was a frog in its place. She felt awkward, embarrassed, but she had to know the answer to the next question. She knew that no one else on their two-way code could listen in.

'Do you . . . well . . . do you . . . sort-of remember anything of the night, Jard? I mean, it's not important . . . except it was a bit cold. Over.'

'No, I don't remember that . . . except seeing someone close by. A face, or something. I think it was early in the morning. Just a flash picture, but I thought it was yours. I could be wrong. The next thing I knew I was in the hospital.'

So that was all!

Mardie was so relieved she slumped in her chair.

'Oh, it was probably one of the men. Or Mister Falldown.'

'It wasn't Mister Falldown. It was a white face . . . if there was one there at all. I could have imagined it. Of course Joanna was there some time. Yes – I remember that now. Things come back bit by bit. She was peering into my eyes. I remember her face close to mine then. Other people around – that sort of thing.'

'She did give you a thorough search and run-over, Jard. You know, the usual First Aid stuff. She's awfully good at it.'

'Yes. But there was something else about a face. Forget it, shall we? I guess I was dreaming. That is, if people can *dream* in a half-conscious state.'

'That would be it, of course,' Mardie said hastily. 'Anyhow, Mister Falldown and later Joanna did all sorts of wonder things for you. They both seemed to know *how*. I'm afraid I wasn't much use then.'

'Don't be modest, Mardie. You did a wonderful job to get me out of that 'copter. Let me thank you for that again. As soon as I can use a car or if one of the men is going over for stores, I'll come and thank you personally. That is, if I may? You might be harbouring hard feelings about my part in the accident. I did wreck you. Over to you again.'

'Oh no! No! No hard feelings, Jard. The opposite. Please do come when you can. But just to visit us. There's nothing to thank me for. You must go and see Mister Falldown for that. Over.'

'I'll be seeing you both. By the way, how's Digger?'

'He's fine, too. He had medical attention from the pilot. You should be asking after Dingo Pup.'

'I have. At least Mister Falldown has sent messages by way of a couple of tribesmen. Dingo Pup is fine, growing, and being firmly taught by Mister Falldown that killing other animals is not the in-thing this year. Over now, Mardie. Thank you once again, and I'll be across to see you as soon as possible.'

'Goodbye, Jard. Over and out – '

Mardie's last words had the cadences of a dying fall, the descending seventh. She could hardly bear to put the mouthpiece back on its hook.

So he doesn't remember the night. Nor what went on *through* the night. Thank God very, very much for that!

Yet somehow it was sad. Something one fine cold night had happened in her life, and now must be lost. Gone for ever.

Except perhaps when she was old, grey-haired – a grandmother sitting in an armchair – she could then begin to tell the children her story . . .

Once in a wild brown empty land a strange thing happened . . .

Of course she would have to marry someone, somewhere, some day. Otherwise she could never be a grandmother. And the story would never be told. But who would come? And when? She supposed that was every girl's question.

Mardie pushed her fingers through her hair. Then she pulled her account books towards her.

It's funny how work never stops, she thought. She bent her head and began adding figures to figures to make neat columns. She always *did* like neat columns.

'That reminds me.' She jumped up and went running to the door. 'Those bricklayers and the spirit level! I'd better keep my eye on *them*. And they'd just better not say they've mislaid the thing again.'

Anything to take her mind off glad things that were sometimes sad things – like falling down from the sky in a cracked-up 'copter, alone with a man whose image she could not get out of her mind.

It was two weeks later that two men came to The Breakaway. *The* two men! The runaways!

Mardie was talking to her builder, screened from the outside world by a head-high brick wall and a glass window about to be fitted into its wall space. Beyond the builder's burly figure she saw the station waggon turn into the west side of The Breakaway and park under the trees.

More through-travellers, she thought, and went on running her fingers down the vertical line of the window frame.

'There's a space there wide enough to see through,' she began. Then stopped short.

Through the space between the window frame and the unfinished brick wall she saw the driver get out of the station waggon on one side, then his passenger heft himself out from the far seat. They met at the rear of the car. They paused to make a few remarks about the new motel units, and as they did so they looked straight in Mardie's direction.

It wasn't their hats, their clothes, their hands or their boots she recognized. Those things were all too neat and spruced up for that. It was their faces.

She had seen these two men before. They had been dusty and hairy then. But she knew them, mostly because of the eyes. And their expressions. They had each carried a rifle in that before-time, and she had thought they were dingo-shooters, maybe. The morning light had been no more than grey shimmer of false dawn, but they had looked down at her. And they had recognized Jard. They had turned about and gone, faster than they came. They had given no help to the injured man lying beside Mardie, and they had not sent back help from wherever it was they went.

She had looked up – that time – pleading, right into their faces and she had seen their eyes. And the expressions in them.

Now, this day, Mardie stood statue still, a warning hand on the builder's arm, and watched these two men standing some distance away, appraising the new brick building rising along the line of trees at the far side of The Breakaway. She remembered that it had been when they had looked down on herself and Jard lying on the ground, Jard had first opened his eyes and looked at her. Right at her. He had looked into her eyes, and the two men had seen his face and recognized him. Then *scrammed*. Jard had not later remembered anything about it. She had not told him about it on the two-way. But David knew about them. She had told him.

'Mr Evans,' she said in a low voice, dropping her hand from the builder's arm. 'If those two men come closer, keep them talking, but don't tell them *anything* except maybe about building things. Not about anything at all. *Please.* Not about me or the Richies, or who and what visitors come to The

Breakaway. You understand? It's important.' The builder nodded. 'Tell them nothing,' Mardie repeated. 'You know nothing except you're the contractor up from the south to put up this building. You know nothing about anybody or anything. Promise me?'

He nodded. 'Just as you say, Miss Forrester. I know there's trouble outback these days what with the mining and strangers coming in for a share in the stakes. I guess they're not your regulars, eh?'

'They're not, but keep them talking, please – about bricks and mortar or window frames that don't always fit. Anything that has nothing to do with the district or anyone in it. As soon as I slip out behind the rear wall, keep their attention in this direction. I want to get across to the main building without being noticed. And I want ten minutes there before they come in for stores or drinks or whatever it is they want. Can you hold them up for ten minutes?'

'Okay, Miss. You're the boss round here. What you say goes. I'll keep 'em talking. Or maybe just plain looking. I'll give 'em a sight-seeing tour. How's that?'

'Thank you.'

She slipped to the back wall, then out through the opening for the future doorway. Once outside she glanced back over the half-wall and saw that Mr Evans had gone out to the two men. He was pointing to something on the west side beyond the station waggon as if telling them the problems of trucking up building materials from the south, or some such.

Mardie ran the few yards into the rear part of the store.

'Mrs Richie!' She was all but breathless. 'There are two men out there who've just pulled in. They came in a station waggon. When they come in, will you keep them in the bar as long as you can? Offer them everything under the sun to keep them here – drinks, food, chatter. Spoil them with attention. *Please.* I'll explain later. But don't tell them about *me* – not even that I'm here. I want to get across to the office and call the Dig-in. The longer you can keep them here – hours if possible – the better. I'll make myself some tea over in the office.'

Mardie slid crabwise along the wall of the bar towards the front entrance and peered out. The men were not in sight. They were still on the far side of the main Breakaway building, being held in thrall, Mardie prayed, by Mr Evans's building problems in the outback. She made doubly sure there was no sound of oncoming boots – no sign of approaching men casting their shadows before them as they walked. Then she slipped across the cement way under the trellis and into her office.

She closed the door and for no reason she could think of at the moment, or at any time later, she locked it. She crossed to the two-way fixture beside the wall table, then lifted the mouth-piece from the hook and pressed the code button for the Dig-in.

'Red Wine answering. Over.'

It was David Ashton.

'Bickleys Brandy, David. Oh, David darling, I'm so glad it's you and not one of the others. Where's Jard Hunter just now? Is he at the out-camp or somewhere up on the water-track?'

'Thank you for the "darling", darling. Remind me to kiss you for that next time we meet. Jard's at the out-camp but I can get him on our out-camp code if it's anything important. Over.'

'I don't know whether it's important or something that's really urgent. Can you keep listening, and is there no cut-in on the wave length anywhere? Over.'

'I can keep listening. There's no cut-in unless some outsider knows the code. We don't use the Red Wine for any contact except to The Breakaway. Go ahead, Mardie.'

'You remember about the two men who came out of the bush just before dawn when Jard was still unconscious after the crash? It was a few minutes before Mister Falldown arrived. Over.'

'Yes. They cleared off without giving you any assistance. You said they recognized Jard. Were you certain about that?'

'Yes. They said his name. Then bent down to look at his face and I saw their faces distinctly. Their eyes mostly. That was because I was pleading with them. That's when you look straight into people's eyes, isn't it? Don't cut out, David. I'll finish what I'm saying first. *They're here at The Breakaway*. Outside talking to Mr Evans, the builder. They're dressed differently . . . sort-of more like ordinary through-travellers. Not so outbackish. They're neater. And they're not carrying rifles this time. If they have rifles they'd be in the station waggon. When I told you about the men before, you said – in a serious way – *Jard would be looking for them.* I mean *you* spoke as if you knew who they might be, and that you distrusted them. Over.'

'Don't get worried about them at this stage, Mardie, but answer two questions if you can. Have they seen you yourself? If so, have they recognized you? Over.'

'They haven't seen me except at a distance. I don't know if they would recognize me or not, as after all I'm upright and day-dressed now. When they came through the bush they sort-of looked at Jard – said his name – then made off. Over.'

'Listen carefully, Mardie. Let them see you, and don't be scared about them. If they are the men we think they are, they've everything to do with mining exploration, and that's all I'm saying for the moment. Their rifles would be for game-hunting. That's their front cover. We at the Dig-in want to catch up with them. Jard especially. So see if you can get the Richies to inveigle them to stop over at The Breakaway. You know – one of those three timber rooms at the back where the truckies put up. If you yourself deal with them, treat them casually, the same way as you treat the usual stop-overs. I can promise you they won't harm anyone at The Breakaway. They're not that type. It's Jard's business they've stuck their noses into. Can do? Over.'

'Can do all right, David, but it won't be easy for *me* to treat them as well as we treat our usual customers. They left me and Jard to perish out there in the bush – so I don't love them any. But I'll try.'

'You don't have to love them, sweetheart. Keep all the loving for me. I'm the one on the waiting list. Just keep them entertained – or whatever it is you do for stop-overs. The thing is to keep them there till I can get in touch with Jard. Don't let them near your office because they might pick up our call-signs, or pinch the code book. If they're the men I think they are they'll give their immortal souls for the code book. If they're not our interest, then there's nothing lost. Okay?'

'I'll tell Mrs Richie to charge them double on account of deserting us in our hour of need – meaning Jard mostly.'

David's laugh was soft and endearing.

'You can make the bill triple if they're our boys. Meantime keep it in mind that you just might be mistaken. Light at false dawn can be misleading. What makes you think they don't look outbackish now? Over.'

'Too neat. City casual wear – as if they're *playing* at being through-travellers. But their faces and hands are burned brown like everyone else living out here.'

'You sound very certain.'

'I am. You don't forget those faces and those eyes when they belong to two men who desert you.'

David's voice was still quiet and reassuring. He even put in a mild laugh – perhaps to comfort her.

'Well, sweetheart, in spite of such churlish treatment you and Jard are still alive and kicking, so don't chew on it too hard. If they're not our men, they're harmless. If they are, we'll catch up now. That is, if you can hang on to them long enough. Will do?'

I was thinking about Jard not being alive and kicking, not me, Mardie thought. She could hardly say that over the air to David. After all, Jard was Joanna's possession. Was or wasn't he? Not anyone – not David nor anyone else must ever know just how she, Mardie, had felt about Jard that night. Nor how she had held him and kept him warm . . .

'You still on the air, Mardie?' David's voice came through.

'Yes. I was just thinking. I'm not scared of the men harming me. I'll harm them first – and mean it. But you're sure the Richies will be all right? Over.'

'Absolutely sure. Down south, at home in their suburban boxes, that pair are sweet-living, law-abiding citizens. Up here's different. You with me?'

'Yes, David, if you say so.'

'The only thing to remember is not to let them near your office, and that code book, or any code at all. Lock such things up in your safe. Enough for now, Mardie love. You'll get a call from Jard as soon as I can contact him. Keep smiling. Love to the Richies. Over and out.'

'Over and out,' Mardie said softly. But of course David didn't hear that. He had already cut from the air.

TEN

Mardie took the Richies into her confidence, and all three of them put their heads together as to methods by which to make the two men welcome when they came into the store. Mr Richie busied himself pouring them very, very generous drinks, and Mrs Richie offered them lunch.

'I've something special,' she said with a broad smile – not mentioning she'd taken it out of the deep freezer only five minutes before. 'You're lucky. We only have our special recipe for brush-turkey one day a month. Today's the day.'

'Brush-turkey, hey?' the taller man said with a grin. 'You must have been out moon-lighting, Missis. It's against the law to kill brush-turkey up this way, isn't it?'

'Yes. But we didn't kill it, you see. It was brought in by one of the station owners passing through. I don't ever ask questions when things like this come my way. What did you say your name was, please?'

'I didn't say, but I'm Jim and my mate's name is Bill. Smith and Brown are the surnames.'

'Jim Smith. Bill Brown. I seem to have heard names like that before.' Mrs Richie was busy rinsing glasses while her husband filled up for the visitors. 'I must have read those names in a book. You wouldn't be famous people, would you?'

'I guess you're a very literary person, Missis. Smith and Brown are real pedigree names. Now what about that brush-turkey? Eh, Bill? Sounds good to me.'

'If you're thinking of staying overnight I'll need those two pedigreed surnames for the register,' Mr Richie said cheerfully. 'What's the hurry, anyway? Stay the night, have an early breakfast, and you'll make the Swan River in time for tea tomorrow afternoon.'

Mr Richie had doctored the beers with a modicum of pure alcohol.

Not enough to put them on their ears, he reassured himself. Just enough to keep 'em affable and wide open to suggestion.

Mardie was in the next room all this time – the one on the far side of the pressed iron wall that did not reach the ceiling. Her special job for this occasion was listening-in. Voices rise, and even the row of shining brasses and the fern baskets wouldn't keep out a word that was said in the bar. Mr Richie meantime was hoping Mardie did not possess the sixth sense that would inform her about the pure alcohol. She was too much an innocent to know about that kind of double-dealing ruse.

'You must be pretty keen on business round here,' the man called Bill said. 'Almost begging us to put up for the night. Do you treat all through-travellers to this "Welcome-and-stay" technique?'

Oh dear. Perhaps Mr Richie's overdone it, Mardie feared. She need not have worried. Mr and Mrs Richie were old hands at handling odd customers.

'As many as will listen,' Mrs Richie said. 'And they always come back for more. You see, there's only one way to teach people what a good place this is. That is, give them a taste of it. Clean sheets, hot water, early-morning call with a cup of tea brought in. And . . .'

'And brush-turkey some station owner delivered just by chance,' Jim finished. 'Such enterprise deserves patronage. Specially as you have a point about being able to make the Swan by tea-time tomorrow. Seven hundred miles is a bit far in one go, after all. Eh, Bill?'

Mr Richie nodded sagely, refilling the glasses once again.

'And no other stop-over till you get bang on this side of the Darling Ranges, Mr Smith!' he said. 'By the time you get there, you think you might as well finish the next sixty miles and get home after midnight. A bad mistake that. You know something? There's more accidents going down the Bindoon Hill on the last stage late at night than any place else from north to south. It's steep, it winds, and the driver's three parts asleep . . . worn out with travelling. Should have stopped over – best at The Breakaway, of course – and had a good night's rest before he ever got as far as the Range.'

The two men looked at one another. Mr Richie guessed the extra drops of pure alcohol were working. The visitors seemed amenable to suggestion.

'Tell you what?' He capped his case. 'We got the nicest waitress-cum-housemaid this side of the black stump. She'll look after you. The prim and proper type, mind you. We wouldn't have any other. No nonsense in our stop-over. But she'll make it more pleasant for you to eat the turkey, and later find yourselves waking up to that early-morning cup of tea – when called. *Good service.* That's our motto and what gets us our good name.'

Bill shrugged his shoulders. 'It's the bit about that flaming Bindoon Hill that settles it,' he said. 'Nothing to do with housemaids or turkeys. Weather report from Perth says it's raining down there, and I don't fancy that Bindoon Hill at two in the morning when it's a slippery slide.'

Mardie, on the far side of the wall, gave a sigh of relief. How cunning can we all get? she wondered. She was not only discovering a new side to herself but also new aspects of Mr and Mrs Richie as business managers for The Breakaway. One lives and learns! she thought, a trifle ruefully.

She slipped out through the far door and across to her office.

She locked the door behind her. And then put the code call through to Red Wine. David Ashton came over the air immediately.

'Bickleys Brandy here,' she said, giving the code name.

'Red Wine answering, Mardie. I've been sitting glued to this so-and-so chair for nearly an hour. What luck? Over.'

'They're being chatted along by the Richies in the bar. They're staying for a meal, and what's better, they're staying the night.'

'Holy smoke! Who's worked the miracle over there? It sounds too easy. Over.'

'You've been out here longer than I have, David, but seems you haven't learned everything about Mr and Mrs Richie yet. I couldn't see what they were doing, but I could *hear* them. They have their own brand of miracle-making for winning *some* people over.'

David's laugh was so knowing Mardie wrinkled her brow in thought. What goes on? she wondered. She did not ask aloud for David's next words made her heart miss a beat.

'You won't be getting any air-call from Jard,' he said. 'You'll get him personally. He's on his way now. You should see his dust in another hour.'

'But his leg? He's not risking driving yet, is he?'

'No. Joanna's taking him. She says she has private personal business to do at The Breakaway, anyway. Needless to say, they've taken two of our roustabouts along with them to give might to their right arms. It just could be a party, Mardie. By that last, I mean trouble. In which case, you and the Richies are to get right out of sight. Immediately. Understand? Over.'

'But Joanna's with them! What about Joanna . . . if there's trouble?'

'Joanna can look after herself. Not to worry, Mardie. My private guess is that *her* private business is to see *she's* there to mend any wounds if Jard collects again. But joking apart, I'm fairly sure there'll be trouble. You have your builders on hand. Have the two men recognized you? Over.'

'They haven't seen me yet. When I cut out the call I'll go over and make their acquaintance as The Breakaway's housemaid, believe it or not. Table-waiting thrown in as a side line.'

David's ready laugh was like a roll of gay notes across the ether.

'Richie strategy!' he said. 'Well, well! Don't crawl into bed with either of them, sweetheart, will you? And Joanna wouldn't let you crawl in with Jard, so I think you'll come out of the occasion with your fair name intact. Over and out now. I've the electrical engineer and two mechanics waiting outside wanting to see me. Something bunged up, I suppose. We all have our troubles. 'Bye, love.'

' 'Bye, David. Out.'

Mardie went in for a lot of 'Yes, Mrs Richie' and 'No, Mr Richie' in as meek a voice as possible – all to convince the two strangers of her pseudo-subservient status at The Breakaway. When she had first gone into the dining-room with steaming plates of brush-turkey plus 'vegs for two', she had kept her head down. But, as she turned away after placing the dishes, she was sure the one called Jim Smith stared at her rather keenly. As she neared the door she looked in the sideboard mirror and saw him lean across the table and say something in an undertone to the other man. She went through the door, not waiting to see if Mr Brown also turned to look at her.

'I'm more than ever certain it's *the* two men,' she whispered to Mrs Richie. Voices carried easily through the pressed iron wall between the dining-room and the kitchen. 'I think the Jim Smith one recognized me . . . but I'm not quite sure.'

'Give them ten minutes to mop up that turkey, then go back – see if there's anything else they'd like before I turn on peaches and cream, both tinned. That's all they'll get for dessert if they're a couple of baddies. But don't mention the "tinned" part. That's bad for business. Let them find out for themselves.'

'Oh, but . . .'

'No fresh fruit for *them*. They didn't help you, did they? Hold your head up, Mardie, and let the other one get a good look at you. Don't give any sign that *you* recognize either of them. Mr Richie's gone to stow their bags in the truckies' room. After that he'll disconnect the battery in their station waggon. They can't make a quick getaway that way.'

'But that's illegal, isn't it?' Mardie began.

'So's abandoning people in the bush. That's inhuman,

which is worse. By the time they smell a rat – if they do – Jard and his pals ought to be here, or near.'

Mrs Richie seemed a different person altogether. Mardie was almost fascinated by watching this change. She did not realize the tiger in Mrs Richie's womanly heart had not been roused by Jard's plight on that night, but that of someone who had become her *own* child – Mardie herself.

'Do you think I should say anything to the builders?' Mardie asked, still blinking at the sudden change in The Breakaway's usual comfortable atmosphere.

'Mr Richie'll look after that. Maybe not till Jard gives one or other of us the nod. Don't look so worried, Mardie, we aren't doing anything *wrong,* you know. We're just doing what many in the outback have to do nowadays since the mining boom has brought all sorts of oddies up here.'

Mr Richie came in through the door at that moment.

'Not that much out of the ordinary either, sad to say,' he finished for his wife. 'There's plenty of baddies round these days – not just this pair. It's kindergarten stuff to what it was in the old gold-mining days. Those days it was gold-stealing. Real murder done more than once, even round these parts. There's old abandoned spec' mines not five miles from here and tales can be told about *them*, I can tell you. These days it's claim-jumping, over-pegging someone else's claim, spying for the rumour-mongers down at the Stock Market.'

Mrs Richie nodded her head.

'I'm sure it's something to do with that sort of thing that's made Jard Hunter interested in our Mr Smith and Mr Brown. The way those shares on the Stock Market go up and down like a yo-yo. often on false information! It's a crying shame.'

Mardie, easier now, laughed as she dished tinned peaches into two small bowls.

'You wouldn't believe it,' she said, 'but when I first came here I thought Jard was the mystery man and perhaps *he* had something to do with exploration spying.'

She looked up. The smile disappeared from her face, for Mr and Mrs Richie were standing quite still *staring at her.* Not a muscle moved on either face.

She felt her own face flush from ear to ear. 'Well . . . I was sort-of . . . only joking . . .' she began lamely. Then added defensively: 'But he is something of a mystery – the way he comes and goes.'

'It's to do with his work,' Mr Richie said bluntly. 'Everyone knows some facts, but not *all the facts,* about the Dig-in. He has to watch what he does, where he goes, and why. He's exploring something special. The others out there at the Dig-in are drilling already. Percussion drilling only, of course. That's exploring the mineral zone. But everyone knows what for and where they're doing it and why. The informers want to know *more.* How *much* are they finding and is it high grade or low grade.'

'And Jard's presence in the area raises speculation sky-high,' Mrs Richie put in. 'If there's to be a mine, then they need water. So if the Dig-in's after water already, then *what*? They say any mine needs a million gallons of water – enough to drive a car one hundred and forty times round the world – to put in and run a real mine.'

Mr Richie polished a glass to breaking-point. He threw the pieces in the waste-bin and picked up another one.

'The chaps who move around in the bush nearby are the ones that need watching,' he said. 'They want to know what's in the drill pipe when it comes up. And how much. And why there's a "water" man already at work. And where. Maybe they want to shift "claim pegs" and stick their own pegs in instead – if they think there's a good nickel strike likely. Maybe they think it *is* likely *because* the Dig-in have got a "water" man exploring already. They're *speculating* – that's the word.'

'Sometimes they *sell* information,' Mrs Richie said. 'When it leaks out, up goes the Stock Market balloon sky-high.' She sounded very matter-of-fact. Evidently she was used to this sort of situation. 'Which reminds me – ' She turned to her husband. 'When Jard comes in, don't forget to tell him that big dump-package has arrived for him. You know the thing marked "Impact-Drill – Petrol-driven". That makes good business news for the store, Mardie. If they're going to start using petrol-driven drills we'll have to increase our orders from the oil company. Big orders!'

'Now who's using "inside information"?' Mr Richie demanded. 'And *speculating*?'

'Mardie, love, you'd better take those peaches and cream to our guests,' Mrs Richie said, for once ignoring her husband. 'We don't want them coming out here looking for it. Don't forget to hold your head up this time and let them both take a good look at you.'

'I won't,' Mardie assured her as she carried the bowls of fruit doorwards.

Jard and his party arrived not long afterwards. Mardie was sure – from the manner of the two men – that they recognized her. The Bill Brown one was not quite so certain. Maybe this was because it had been false dawn that morning of the 'copter crash and his sight wasn't as keen. Maybe he had been too busy recognizing Jard. She probably had had strands of hair falling over her face. Besides, she hadn't had any clothes on to speak of, had she? She was glad she had done what she had done. It had helped Jard. But how was she to live with it once she saw him again and remembered those long hours through the night?

She watched the Dig-in's utility turn in to The Breakaway, then stop in a situation that crowded the station waggon. Mr Richie had gone out earlier and asked the builder to back down one of his trucks so it, too, was now parked under the trees alongside the fence and only a foot in front of the station waggon. Meantime Mrs Richie was keeping Mr Smith and Mr Brown talking in the bar over a strong liqueur. 'On the house,' she had said, adding that this was because they were staying guests. The usual thing. Alongside each man also stood a cup of black coffee.

'No meal of my cooking is complete without a liqueur and coffee to follow,' she had said. 'We do things properly at The Breakaway. That's why our customers come again. It's good for trade to treat customers well.'

The one called Jim may have had special thoughts about Mardie but the good meal and those little doses of pure alcohol surreptitiously slipped in the men's beer earlier – topped off now with a noble Drambuie liqueur – were matters that worked their charm. He lounged one elbow on the bar counter and quizzed his hostess on the subject of The Breakaway's customers.

'Plenty of those mining blokes about,' he supposed. 'What are they all up to round these parts? Everyone knows they've had something of a nickel strike out at the Dig-in. It was all in the papers. But how much and what's it worth? That's the thing, eh, Missis?'

Bill Brown, less loosened up, was more guarded. Mrs Richie had been well aware he had given his mate a kick on the shins on the far side of the bar counter. But she made no sign. She addressed herself exclusively to Jim. He was the one she must keep talking – even if it meant leaning on her highly polished bar – till Jard arrived.

'Well, everyone asks questions,' she said, shrugging. 'Like you, I only read what's in the papers. I'm for always wondering why those that wants to know don't go out to the Dig-in and ask. There's a well-worn track out there . . . so I'm told.'

'Huh! They'd be same as the rest of the type. Keep a guard on the place. Warn off callers. Scared stiff someone might jump their claim, I guess, or take a quick snook at their plastic sample bags. Even read the labels.'

'Well, that's been done . . . so I read in the papers,' Mrs Richie shrugged again as she refilled the coffee cups. She didn't like her visitors well enough to give them a second liqueur 'on the house'. That Drambuie stuff cost money and she wouldn't care to put a bill in to the Dig-in because of it. After all, the Dig-in were good customers. Likely to be better, too, with them taking up those petrol-driven drills. All she had to do right now was keep these men talking. That was what Mr Richie had said. And Mardie had agreed.

Jim and Bill drank the coffee while they eyed the Drambuie back on the shelf.

Mrs Richie's sharp ears had caught new sounds in the distance. Under her apron she crossed her fingers. Let this be Jard, she thought. Then he can take over from here. So long as they keep Mardie out of the fire-line.

Mrs Richie had her own views as to what kind of bullets might come Mardie's way and they weren't bullets from fire-arms, that was for sure. Mardie had told her a little . . . a very, very little . . . of that night after the 'copter crash, but her diffidence in telling and the high colour that had suffused her face while the words came stilted, had told a tale of their own. Mrs Richie had done a little guessing, and her concern now was that the girl would come to no harm because of that nightly vigil.

If these two men – right baddies in her estimation – really recognized Mardie as the girl on the ground with Jard, well then, they could make something of it, couldn't they?

Mardie saw the Dig-in ute swing round at a hot pace and stop, slightly angled, close behind the station waggon. If Mr Smith and Mr Brown went for their vehicle they couldn't back it out. It was parked-in. The builder's truck in front, and the ute behind. The station waggon could neither move forward nor back out.

When the ute slammed to a halt Mardie stopped thinking about the two men in the bar. She didn't even look at Joanna in the front seat beside Jard, or the two roustabouts sitting on oil drums in the tray. She looked only at Jard.

He was someone different now. He was a man with whom she had spent one long, cold, memorable night. Someone who had – for one short space in time – belonged to her.

They all four, including Joanna, tumbled out of the ute simultaneously. One of the roustabouts stayed with it. He leaned with his backside against the bonnet, his arms folded and his dead-pan face watching the others move across the ward to the trellised way.

Mr Richie, outside talking to the builder, walked quietly towards the rear entrance of The Breakaway. The builder moved over to the station waggon as if looking it over in the casual manner of a man who might be thinking of buying something like it some day.

Mardie watched the scene with a mounting mixture of anxiety and excitement. It all looked like a planned deploying of man-power and a silent imminent invasion.

She shook her head.

But this doesn't happen here, she thought. It's not real. I'm dreaming it. Before any mining boom, the outback was known as so safe.

But it was happening.

This was Western Australia in the same kind of mining boom that had happened at the turn of the century – then gold – and in these same mining areas here at The Breakaway. The only difference was that out there now there were cars and utes and trucks whereas, in those other boom days, there had been horses and camel trains. And even now, Jard, Joanna and the roustabouts didn't carry firearms.

But the way they deployed themselves! And the way they walked – their heads slightly lowered but looking up from under the brims of those hats! Even Joanna in her khaki safari jacket and shorts, her broad-brimmed flop hat, suddenly seemed to look and walk like the men.

One more notch up to Joanna, Mardie thought. Something else she can do. Match it with the men in a take-over.

ELEVEN

Behind the bar counter Mrs Richie heard them coming.

'More through-travellers,' she said in a matter-of-fact voice. 'All good for business. By the sound of those boots they'll be mining men, and they're better spenders, you know. Not used to being left out at those mining camps for long stretches like the station people.'

Jard came through the door, walked casually towards the bar and nodded to Mrs Richie. Jim Smith and Bill Brown were elbow-leaning on the counter and clutching a glass in the spare hand. They turned casually to take in the newcomer.

Suddenly there was something different in the air.

Joanna slipped silently behind the bar and took Mrs Richie's arm. She said one word, *'Out.'*

'Anyone would think this is *your* stop-over,' Mrs Richie said sharply. But nevertheless she went. Joanna took her place.

'Drinks, gentlemen?' she asked, but no one answered her.

The two strangers had straightened up. They held their glasses in their hands almost as if they could, if necessary, use them – broken-ended – as weapons.

Jard and his roustabout stood side by side, their hands tucked in their belts almost in identical stances.

'So? You two called in for a drink?' Jim Smith asked, an edge of care in his voice.

'No. We called in to see you.' Jard's voice was soft, but in a deadly way. His eyes were expressionless. Stony. 'We heard you were round about this area.'

'So what?' There was unease in Bill Brown's expression but a touch of insolence in Jim Smith, who spoke. 'It's a public stop-over, isn't it? The area is crown land whether the station owners lob their homesteads and run their sheep on it, or the mining mob line up their bun-houses round their drill sites. Like it or not.'

'Whatever it is – whoever is squatting – you two put a distance between yourselves and the area. Or else!' Jard's voice was as stony as his eyes.

'Or else what?' Jim Smith was very insolent now. 'You

show me any law that says we're trespassing here . . . any more'n you and your mate there are trespassing right this minute. We've registered for accommodation. Take a look-see for yourselves.'

'Pull the register from under the counter, Joanna,' Jard said. 'Open it at the last page and turn it round so I can see it.' His voice had not altered by a note or a cadence. It was quiet and deadly.

Mardie had been told to stay in her office and out of sight. But she too had a will of her own. She slipped round the back of the building, then came via the kitchen into the dining-cum-sitting-room that was on the far side of the three-quarter wall next to the bar. As of earlier in the day, the polished brasses and the baskets of hanging ferns could not keep out the voices from the other side. She had not *deserted* her office. She had left it with deliberate intention. The Breakaway was *hers.* While Joanna might automatically be included in an invasion party she, Mardie Forrester, was not going to be kept hidden away, an over-protected frail piece of feminity. She not only had a right to be where Joanna was part of the party, she had a *duty* to be where she *belonged.* If anything went wrong then it was on her property.

Mardie had busily marshalled up this sequence of ironclad thoughts while still in the office. She didn't *feel* that way. Only *thought* that way. Her feelings and thoughts were having a war of their own. Everyone wanted her safely out of the way because she might be a liability. She was a novice at this sort of situation. She knew that. But her feelings said – if trouble started she not only had a *right,* but she *wanted* to be here. She had slept beside Jard in the bush that night and those two men in there had recognized her, and knew it. *Jard did not know it.* Dear God . . . what was worse, Joanna did not know it. Not the details of that night. And Jard, so it seemed from appearances, belonged to Joanna. If there were to be explanations, not trouble, coming out in the confrontation next door, she needed to be able to supply some of her own.

If there was trouble only, then in spite of Joanna's expertise she, Mardie, was going to come in on the First Aid deal too. She was *not* going to be the useless little woman tucked off in the office out of harm's way.

Sitting at the table in the room on the wrong side of the wall, her elbows on the table and her chin resting on the backs of her folded hands, she was not so surprised at the steel in Jard's voice but at the softness of it. And the command in the very softness.

She wasn't surprised at her own reaction. It made her heart turn over because now she admitted she had been keeping a near-secret even from herself. She was falling stupidly and blindly from her perch of independence. She was in love with him. And that was that!

Dear heaven! Was it with the man holding to ransom the baddies next door? Or was it that pale face with the bloodstain across the brow that had lain so close to her all that long, cold night? She didn't know. Or care. All she did know was that The Breakaway stop-over was hers. And Jard – that night – had been *her* care too. *Hers.*

So she was *here* where she had a right to be. And her heart was beating its own lonely race – all because of Jard.

Joanna had turned the register round and Jard glanced at it. Then he looked up straight at Jim Smith. Bill Brown was clearly the follower, not the leader, for he spoke not one word.

'Smith and Brown?' Jard's cold voice came through the space between the wall-top and the ceiling. 'What original ideas! *Brian Renton and Philip Sexter,* I charge you, in the presence of two witnesses, with misrepresentation by signing a register in a public stop-over with assumed names – therefore false – and false addresses. More serious, I charge you with being in possession of two rifles not registered with the police or any other properly nominated authority.'

There was dead silence for a moment. Then Jim Smith laughed.

'Who the heck do you think you are?' he demanded. 'Police? Judge and jury? The lot? As for rifles. Search us and search that truckies' dump up the back where our bags are, and see if you find rifles.'

'Look through the door behind you,' Jard said. 'There's a man bringing two rifles across the yard. He's just taken them from your station waggon . . .'

Smith and Brown swung round and stared over Jard's shoulder. The third roustabout from the Dig-in was coming across the cement way carrying the two weapons.

Mardie could not see it, but she guessed Jard all but smiled. He'd made a random guess and guessed right. These drop-ins were the two men who had been at the scene of the 'copter crash and had been carrying rifles then. David Ashton had given him that information from Mardie's description. His *guess* had been they would still have them in their possession. In the interim period between the crash and this now-time he had checked over the radio if Renton and Sexter . . . the two men he knew them to be . . . had registered their rifles with the police.

Mardie – behind her wall – put all the twos and twos together, and took in a breath. How thorough could Jard be! David had said Jard would be interested in these two men and that meant the Dig-in people knew about them, and that they were in the district. Also, that they were up to no good as far as Dig-in affairs were concerned. Mardie's description had tallied with their own foreknowledge of the two men.

What sort of 'baddies' were they? she wondered. Well, she didn't have time to think now.

'As for being police or law,' Jard's voice was steadily going on. 'You are not up with the law yourselves. Any civilian – repeat – *any* civilian may charge another civilian with a legal offence and report the charge to the police. I'll officially report the charge re the rifles, so I suggest you clear out and stay out of the area, because they'll catch up with you. Preferably not *here*.'

Suddenly everyone's attention was distracted by the sound of a powerful-engined car pulling up, car doors slamming, then footsteps crossing the yard. They came on, a heavy man's tread, and the lighter sound of women's footsteps. Three people came along the cement by the trellis, then in through the doorway.

'Hallo, hallo, everybody!' A woman's light, cheerful voice saluted them. 'Joanna . . . nice to see you! And *Jard*! Jard darling, how are you after that awful time you had with the crash? We had our ears glued to the Session listening for news of you, didn't we, Ted?'

Ted – tall, lean, sun-browned to bark colour – was very much the station man. He nodded in agreement with his wife, and shook Jard's hand warmly – as of old friends well met. The second woman, very fair, was younger but with a pretty face seared with tiny wrinkles from too much exposure to the outback sun and heat. She slipped her hand in Jard's arm.

'Hallo, sweetie!' she said. 'Long time no see. What you

been doing, pet? Looking for underground water or finding nickel? You will let us into the big strike come the day, won't you?'

'Everyone round this district is waiting to make his fortune out of you boys at the Dig-in,' the man called Ted said jovially. 'This Mansell family not least. As you darnall know, Jard, we've pegged our own property come the day you fellers want to start sinking drills on it.'

The Mansells, Mardie thought, from next door. Do I or don't I go in now? She thought hard. Did it matter now that she was the one to identify the two men who had been at the crash that early morning? Jard was giving them the go-about on account of the rifles. Wasn't that enough? You can't arrest people for not giving assistance to accident victims – or can you?

From the sounds and chatter next door Joanna was already acting as The Breakaway's hostess. Mardie tried not to feel indignant. The Breakaway was hers. Her very own! Glasses were clinking. Jard's voice could be heard, ushering Smith and Brown doorwards, with a few well-chosen words. Apparently he was not letting the Mansells know they were currently in the company of two district baddies. Did mining men always have to be so secretive?

Mardie stopped thinking and went into action. She moved across to the sideboard drawer – a piece of furniture on the way to being an antique. Nearly a century old. She took out the powder compact she kept hidden at the back of the drawer against emergencies. She did the right things to her face, pushed up her hair to make sure it was neat and tidy, then headed for the glass-clinking society next door.

She tried not to notice that Joanna, amidst much smiling, was pouring drinks for the newcomers – very much in charge. The best Scotch whisky too.

When Mardie came in from the rear doorway, Jard had reached the front entrance with the two men. He was almost shouldering them through it.

'Oh, come in, Mardie dear!' Joanna said – a throwaway invitation over her shoulder. 'All's well now, except for our welcoming your station neighbours from up the track. Mrs Mansell, this is Mardie Forrester.'

Mardie went on trying not to mind that Joanna was still playing the hostess in her, Mardie's, house.

'How do you do, Mrs Mansell,' she said and with her best smile. She turned to the tall sunburned man. 'You must be Mr Mansell?'

'And I'm Sylvie . . . just the sister-in-law,' the younger woman announced.

At the mention of Mardie's name, the 'Jim Smith' man looked back over his shoulder. He knocked his friend Bill Brown with his elbow.

'Look who's here!' he said savagely. 'No wonder Mr Jard Hunter is anxious to show us the way out. That's the girl he was sleeping with in the bush. Recognize her? Not a stitch on, the pair of them, either . . . if I remember rightly.'

'You always had a memory for faces,' Bill Brown said in equally ugly tones. 'For the upper works too, this time. That's the girl-under-the-rug all right.' He gave a short laugh. 'A faked injury as some excuse, eh? A real new one, that. We could add it to our own repertoire.' Revenge seemed very sweet – for the moment.

For one minute the room was frozen in silence. Mardie's flush all but equalled the angry astonishment in Joanna's face. The Mansell party stood and stared, first at Mardie, then at the group in the doorway. Jard's face had gone white with anger. It read as if he was controlling himself to the pitch of extremes.

'*Out*!' he said through half-closed lips to the two men. His voice had the crack of a whip in it. He and the roustabout shouldered the two men outside.

Mardie never did know what really happened next, or the exact manner in which the two men were literally put off the premises. She closed her eyes.

Inside The Breakaway things were different.

'What did that man say?' Joanna asked in a meaningful but quiet voice. She stared at Mardie, right in the eyes. She was demanding an answer from *her*. Not from anyone else in the room.

The Mansells fidgeted with their glasses in a mixture of discomfort, curiosity and disbelief.

Mrs Richie, returning to her own province through the rear door, hustled to the rescue.

'They're baddies,' she said in a matter-of-fact voice. 'Jard put those two men off the premises at *my* request. It sometimes happens, you know. We serve drinks here and, as it's an isolated place, occasional drop-ins get out of hand. But it's very rare, mind you. Very rare indeed. Ever only happened once or twice.'

'Yes . . . but what the dark one said . . . about . . .' Mrs Mansell looked around, puzzled. Her expression was shocked.

Mrs Richie gave Joanna her best smile.

'Thank you, miss, for helping out. I'll take over now.' She turned to Mrs Mansell with her best house-warming smile. 'Men like that pair *have* to say something, you know, if they're put off the premises. They always have an excuse for themselves by putting the *other* person in the wrong. Unpleasant types. Very nasty minds, if you ask me. It takes all sorts to make up the world. Good and bad. Such a pity!'

'But . . .' Sylvia Mansell again had a puzzled expression in both voice and face. 'The Breakaway is not a place like that, is it? I mean, it's more a place for through-travellers and . . . and social meetings. Like today, I mean. Well, like it was meant to be today, that is. Just a call in. The Breakaway . . .'

'Quite right, Miss Mansell.' Mrs Richie's manner was comforting. 'The Breakaway has had a wonderful reputation for three generations. But just now and again, well, once in a blue moon, there might be a nasty type drop in. It was a good job we had Jard and one of his men here today. What with Mr Richie outside settling some matters with the builders. But mind you – you never take any notice of what the unpleasant types say. They say anything that comes into their heads. They have to get their own back as it were. That was because Jard was putting them out, of course.'

'Quite right,' Mr Mansell said. 'Why, over the years we ourselves have had one or two stockmen we've had to deal with pretty firmly. You know that, May. Once it was a jackeroo. And remember what he said? It was poor Sylvie here. Thank God she was in Perth at the time so the feller was proved a liar. No trouble about *that*. Everyone knew where Sylvie was at the time.'

Joanna was looking steadily at Mardie.

'But you weren't in Perth, were you, Mardie?' she asked, her voice demanding an explanation.

'No. I was at the crash. With Jard.' She swallowed the frog in her throat. 'But Mister Falldown came after those two men left. Mister Falldown thought that whatever I had done – First Aid sort-of – was the right thing. He'll say so, I know.'

Mr Mansell came across and put his arm along Mardie's shoulder.

'We don't have to call in the old feller to give you an alibi, Mardie,' he said, giving cheer. 'Forget it, girl. No one will take notice of a pair like that. Two days ago we had the police over the air making inquiries about a couple answering to their descriptions. No-good-'uns, all right. And – like Mrs Richie said – they always have to say something nasty to get their own back. It's routine with that type.'

Alibi? Mardie was thinking. Alibi? But I didn't need an alibi. I haven't got one. I did do that. I did lie close to him . . . like that . . .

She was shocked herself. Bewildered too. And Jard? What would he think? It was only what Jard might think that mattered . . .

Her gaze wandered round the room, seeking yet not seeing. *About these people here . . . it doesn't really matter! Not all that much. But it matters about Jard . ..*

Her thoughts broke off as she met the other girl's eyes. Joanna was clever and she would read the misery in her face. She would interpret it her own way. And, because she was clever and a scientist, she would interpret it the right way. *Joanna would know.*

Joanna did know.

'We'll talk this over later, Mardie,' she said quietly. 'For now I think you'd better have a drink.' Her eyes, very composed, swept round the room. They included Mrs Richie and lingered there just one fraction of a second longer. 'As for the rest of us,' she added, 'perhaps Mrs Richie will give us all a drink. And, of course, we all know that was a load of rubbish we've just heard.' Her glance took them all in again. 'No one in this room even remembers what they said, do we? That's for Jard's sake, of course. We all know he was unconscious. We all heard the news bulletins from the Flying Doctor Service over the air, didn't we?' Her tone was commanding, not asking.

'Oh, of course!' Mrs Mansell relaxed almost too obviously. 'It was just such a shock to hear anyone talk like that, wasn't it? I mean, that's why we all looked so aghast. Now we're all agreed, aren't we? No one in this room ever mentions it again . . . for darling Jard's sake. It could make such mischief!'

'For Mardie's sake too,' Mrs Richie said very quietly.

Sylvie Mansell gave a nervous, brittle sort of laugh. 'Oh *yes*. Of course for Mardie's sake too. After all, a girl's reputation is her most treasured possession, isn't it?'

'What is her most treasured possession?'

Jard was standing in the doorway. His voice was steady.

'Oh, a diamond ring on her left hand, I expect,' Mrs Mansell said thoughtlessly. Then, when she realized what she had said, she flushed. 'I mean jewellery, of course. Or . . . or . . .' she stammered. 'Any kind of jewellery. Women . . . girls . . . do love pretty things, don't they? I mean . . . I do . . .'

'If you will excuse me for a few minutes,' Mardie said coolly, 'I want to speak to the builder before the men knock off.'

She felt Joanna's eyes burning holes in her back. To have turned and gone through the rear door would have beat a retreat. She must go the normal way – through the front entrance. With her head up – high. She did that.

She walked quietly towards the door. To keep up the pretence of dignity she had to lift her eyes and give Jard a wry smile.

He was looking at her steadily, a contained, watchful expression in his eyes. Yet, this time, his eyes were saying something. What? They were no longer cold stone. There was almost compassion in them. It made Mardie's heart turn over, all over again.

Oh why, why, *why* did this have to happen to her?

Will Power, please come to my aid.

It did.

She smiled. She was unaware of a prayer for understanding in it.

He knows I did sleep with him that night. He realizes it had to be true. That it made sense because of the cold. And he's sorry for me.

Sorry! Who wants *pity*!

'Not to worry!' she said, looking straight into his eyes. 'The funniest things happen in the outback, don't they? And get said too! Who'd ever have thought an eagle would attack a 'copter, for instance? Or make such a noise about it? But you wouldn't remember that, would you?'

He stood aside for her to pass through.

'But the eagle *did* attack,' he said. 'Fifteen inches of rain have been known to fall overnight in the middle of the desert too. An earthquake, not known in this continent for millions of years, shook the State and wrecked a whole town. The strangest things *do* happen. I agree.'

Mardie's laugh was genuine. *It was going to be all right.* He was taking it lightly. Her flush died away and the stiffness went out of her conjured-up dignity.

'Wonders will never cease!' she said, and managed a laugh as she went through the door.

TWELVE

Mardie talked to her builder about the window frame and the door frame. About these bricks and those. She tried to keep her mind on what he was telling her because, after all, these were *her* units going up. The cost of them would take all the capital money left to her by her godfather – along with the rights to the property. She had to find and keep a *business* head on her shoulders. And watch the dollars. She would never be able to look Mr Lawson in the face again if she made a mess of it.

If only her heart would stop pounding long enough for her really to hear and digest what the builder was saying.

He was pointing out that Jard's utility had been moved back by the roustabout before he, too, had gone to join 'the mob' in The Breakaway.

'And downy-looking wallops that pair of no-good-'uns looked when they came out and took off in the station waggon. Guess they're the type that look like something that spells trouble,' he said.

'They might have caused trouble,' Mardie said cautiously, 'but the men from the Dig-in got rid of them for us.'

'Those two rifles?'

'I think they probably weren't registered. It was something to do with that. I'm not sure of the details. It was all beyond me. I don't understand much about fire-arms.'

The builder shrugged his shoulders philosophically.

'The pair of 'em have probably been passing themselves off as registered dingo-shooters. The mining people don't like that type around. Mostly they're snooping on what's going on round the drilling sites – waiting for a strike that smells like a goer.'

'Yes. I have had that explained to me. I believe the spy

planes even carry telescopic sighters on them.'

'They have everything – if their employers are rich enough. That pair probably have a big firm behind them.'

Mardie was beginning to wonder if her new life up here really meant establishing motel units, helping run The Breakaway, or somehow getting herself tangled up with mining exploration and their camp followers.

She turned as she heard the steps coming along the cement path by the trellis.

It was Jard, his roustabouts following him. A minute later Joanna came too. She looked around and spotted Mardie, almost hidden behind the builder and by a double stack of bricks. She came towards them with her usual determined manner.

'Mardie, have you two minutes to spare? I wanted to see you about something, but I mustn't keep Jard waiting. He's one frantically busy man, you know.'

This last sounded possessive as if Joanna was his personal and protective secretary. Or something else?

The builder said, 'Excuse me,' and moved away. Mardie came out from behind the brick stack.

'Yes, of course,' she said with a smile. trying to make it as natural as possible. 'It was such a to-do in there it was impossible to say "hallo" to one another properly, wasn't it? But thank you for minding the bar. It was good of you.'

'Nonsense. We wanted Mrs Richie out of the way in case of trouble. Then, my dear infant, you had to come barging into it. You should have left us to handle it, you know. However, there was no *real* trouble to speak of.'

Joanna's eyes had something near a reprimand in them. They were more like those of a schoolteacher talking to a difficult child.

'Well, as it is my property,' Mardie said mildly, but on purpose, 'it was my responsibility, wasn't it?' She was determined the relationship should return to normal friendliness, if possible. Yet make her point. 'I can understand that men wouldn't want women around, but then you came, Joanna. They wanted *you,* so I didn't think females had to be debarred altogether.'

'I work with the men. And I'm experienced. There's a difference, you see. And *experience* – '

'At trouble-shooting? Joanna, you're a real wonder. Don't you ever feel scared?'

'No. You can't work with men and make a ploy at tender

feminine susceptibilities. I'm not exactly all for Women's Lib, but I do believe if you want equality with men in their jobs then that's exactly what it means – *equality*. You take on the same responsibilities. And I'm the official First Aid hand out at the Dig-in. Extra duties and all that, you know.'

Mardie's voice was very quiet. 'But that's what *I'm* doing here. *Being equal.* Running The Breakaway and building my own motel units.'

Joanna laughed almost derisively, but not quite. 'My dear girl! The Richies have been running The Breakaway for years and years. And you have a builder and skilled workers building your units.'

'*Touché*. But I'm learning. And I'm helping. Sort of *overseeing*, if you know what I mean.'

The expression in Joanna's eyes hardened. 'Is that what you were doing in the bushes after the 'copter crash? Overseeing?'

Mardie flushed. 'Jard was unconscious in that 'copter, and later. What would you have done, Joanna? Left him there? He could have died.'

'You do have a point there. But don't dramatize it, my dear child. As for what those two outsider-men said, it was a pack of downright lies, wasn't it?'

'If it was, why give it another thought? They've been run out of the area now, haven't they? Is anyone likely to take any notice of people like that? They must be notorious anyway, or the Dig-in wouldn't have sent you all over here to get rid of them.'

Joanna eyed Mardie thoughtfully.

Mardie met her gaze. She called up her good Will Power again, and did not blink.

Joanna suddenly relaxed. 'So long as no one allows *Jard* to start worrying about it,' she said. 'A man could be put – wrongfully – in a difficult position. I don't think the Mansells will talk, but we do owe it to Jard not to compromise him unjustly. Don't you think?'

'Of course. Don't worry, Joanna. I know you have a duty to protect the Boss. I feel exactly the same. Mainly because he and the Dig-in are amongst our most valued customers. There's nothing more likely to come out of the whole incident. Do let's forget it. It wasn't very pleasant and is best forgotten.'

Joanna smiled. 'Good girl, Mardie. I did think the first time I met you that you had sense. Thank God for that.

Well, sorry I can't keep the men waiting. 'Bye for now.' She turned away – then back again as if having second thoughts. 'I'll give you a call from the Dig-in some time. You must come over when we have our next film show. We have them regularly to give the men some kind of entertainment, other than cards and two-up. A wide screen and a projector are part of our equipment out there. Supper laid on – ad lib!'

'Lovely! Thank you. I'd love to come.'

'Good. I'll speak to David Ashton about it. He sent his love. I think he's really falling for you, Mardie. He's a nice guy so I wouldn't pass him up, unless you have someone with top priority tucked away down south?' This last was more a question than a quip but Mardie did not answer it.

'I'll be seeing you,' was all she said.

'And me you,' Joanna replied cheerfully. She turned away towards the Dig-in's utility. Jard was already in the drive seat. He was leaning his elbow on the steering wheel, cupping his chin in his hand and looking steadily and thoughtfully in front of him.

Not even a wave goodbye?

Mardie wondered about that, sadly.

Time passed so quickly Mardie almost lost count. The units were finished.

Next came the business of interviewing sales representatives from the south who came to quote for furnishings. Mardie had read up her business journals and realized that, if her accommodation venture was to be a success, the units had to match in furnishings with the standard motels in the north-west towns catering for the big mining interests at Mt Tom Price, Karratha and the busy north-west ports shipping out the iron ore. A bigger generator had to be installed at The Breakaway to cater for extra demands such as air-conditioning as well as better electric lighting.

Because of these affairs Mr Lawson made another flying call to The Breakaway.

Mardie had earlier been anxious about his reaction. She had all the confidence in the world about The Breakaway's future. So many, many people passing through had been delighted at the prospect of having a real modern stop-over. And they had said so warmly. The old truckies' accommodation at the back of The Breakaway could be repaired or pulled down.

There were so many decisions to be made and Mr Lawson since he was the trustee of the estate, had to be consulted.

'Well done, Mardie!' he said as he looked over the units. She was so relieved she could have cried. 'And your book-keeping is a wonder to behold. You went to a good business college, that's clear.'

'Thank God for that,' she said, hugging his arm.

'You can also thank God for being blessed with brains too, my child.'

Mardie's eyes widened. 'Brains?' she said. 'Me? You ought to see what Joanna Seddon can do. She's one of the geologists at the Dig-in. Had a First Aid training too. The only woman . . .'

'Yes. I know all about Joanna. She could run the country – given a chance. A good-looker into the bargain. She has managed to keep her femininity along with it. Quite a girl is Miss Seddon.' Mr Lawson seemed to be indulging in a very private sort of smile.

'Yes. Quite a girl,' Mardie agreed gently.

Mr Lawson glanced at her. 'Do I detect a note of sadness? I thought you admired her?'

'Oh, I do. Tremendously. I guess I'm just envious because I can't do *all* the things she can do.'

'Like what?'

'Talk about things in scientific terms to scientists, to begin with,' Mardie said with a laugh. 'That's a foreign language to simple people like me. I almost feel a dim-wit when the mining people call in. They talk about gossans and costeans. Pre-Cambrian to Mesozoic granites . . . Did you know that that is what this area is in geological age, Mr Lawson? *Pre-Cambrian*?'

'You're learning, aren't you, Mardie? No one can learn things like that in a day.'

'I listen. And I've bought a book. You see, I want to catch up with . . .' she hesitated.

'With whom?' He was watching her face with extra interest.

She looked away as if trying to identify something . . . which was nothing . . . in the distance.

'Well, with them all. I mean, they come in here for stores, you know. And they sit talking. I sort-of wish I could join in . . .'

'Them? Who are they precisely?'

'Oh, Joanna. David Ashton. Lots of the other men from

out there. And . . .' She broke off. She was aware that Mr Lawson was looking at her in a not so usual way.

'And who?' he asked.

Something in her bones told her the name for which he had been waiting.

'There's Jard Hunter, of course.' She said the name casually. This was hard for her. It was hard even to think of him casually. Mr Lawson was too experienced in reading, not only law, but people.

'There is something special about Jard Hunter, isn't there, Mardie? Is it because of the night of the crash?'

Mardie looked in other directions. She did not want to meet his eyes.

'Well . . . naturally.' She made a good attempt at sounding casual. 'We were together in a very nasty accident. No one could forget that, could they? Also he happens . . .' She broke off. Something had clicked with her. Mr Lawson's words . . . 'Because of *the night* of the crash'. There had been the faintest underlining of the words – '*the night*' and not so much of – 'of the crash'. It ought to have been the crash that mattered. *Not* the night.

She looked straight at him, meeting his eyes.

'Who has been telling you about it, Mr Lawson? What have they been saying?'

'This is one of the reasons I have come up to see you, Mardie. I knew how your motel units were coming along. Naturally I had to take a business interest in them. But there was this other matter. Shall we go inside and talk about it? Perhaps Mrs Richie will be kind enough to make us some tea.'

'Yes, of course.'

They walked in silence past the bright-coloured creepers lining the trellis, in through The Breakaway's main entrance, to the sitting-room on the far side of the bar wall.

'Tea please, Mrs Richie. Can you manage it? Mardie and I have much to talk about. Tea always helps, don't you think?'

'Well, with *some*.' Mrs Richie was being philosophic again. 'With others it's a glass of beer or a good stiff whisky. Sure you wouldn't like a whisky – scotch, Mr Lawson?'

'No. Tea please, Mrs Richie. Perhaps we could have a drink together before dinner tonight. That is, if you and Mr Richie will join us. We also have some business to talk about, don't we?'

'Jard Hunter coming in to see you this time, Mr Lawson?'

Mrs Richie asked. But Mardie thought there was something extra in her tone. Maybe it was just that she herself was on guard; sick with doubts. Even anxieties, when it came to mentioning Jard's name. This specially when coupled with the re-telling of the 'copter crash incident. It had been a talking point with the through-travellers for weeks. Its importance had grown out of all proportion to the facts. Two eagles had now become a covey of them. The crippled 'copter had become a complete burn-out. One injured person had now become someone crippled for life. Oh! How that story had altered and grown, finally to become unreal with the re-telling of it!

Mr Lawson and Mardie, seated in the sitting-room, talked about eagles in general and 'copters in particular till Mrs Richie brought in the tea. She made her usual bright contributions to the conversation, then departed, closing the door firmly behind her. Clearly she thought her 'dear child' was now in proper hands.

Mardie poured the tea.

'Why did you want to talk to me about the crash?' she asked as she brought him his tea. Their eyes met and this time Mardie's did not flinch. She wanted to know. The truth . . . whether it hurt or not.

'I think Jard Hunter would like to come and see you about it, Mardie,' he said quietly. 'I happen to be his legal adviser amongst other things. But that has little to do with it. My concern at the moment is with *you.* I think he has something special he would like to discuss with you. I'm the note in the cleft stick – the old primitive way of the messenger bringing the news.'

He took a lump of sugar from the bowl Mardie offered, and looking down at his cup stirred the tea vigorously.

'Yes?'

'My concern is for you, Mardie. Not Jard.' Mr Lawson was being very paternal now. Not legalistic. 'I think you should know, in advance, what he has in mind.'

'But what could he have in mind? It's all over now. It's something in the *past.*'

'But not forgotten.'

'For goodness' sake! He doesn't feel all grateful – or something? I couldn't bear that. All it was was a case of both of us *preserving* ourselves.' That earlier phrase of Mr Lawson's rang in her mind – *the night of the crash.* There was a slight tremor in her hand as she stirred the milk into her own tea. 'Jard couldn't possibly believe the implications of what those two hateful men have said,' she went on. 'He *knows* he was unconscious. What does he fear? Or suspect? That I . . .?' She couldn't go on. She felt her cheeks burning. Alas! She couldn't hide *that* from Mr Lawson. Yet his expression was kindly. Concerned. It all but brought tears to her eyes.

She wasn't so very alone now. There had been her godfather, and he was dead. He had loved her. Mr Lawson had stepped into his shoes. He was being kind. She wanted to forget that awful *alone* period of her life when her mother died, and her father had remarried.

'Please go on,' she said in a steady voice. 'I know there is something you want to tell me. Something important.'

'Important because of my feeling for you, Mardie. I have great admiration for your energy and enterprise up here at The Breakaway. For your thoroughness. And for something more. For *yourself*.'

'Thank you.' Her voice was so low she could hardly hear it herself.

'I also think you have courage. So you must have the courage to listen now. There are matters I believe you should know.'

'Please go on.'

'Very well. I'll begin ahead of events. I know Jard Hunter very well, Mardie. I will sum him up in one sentence. He is a very fine man. He can be a tough man, if necessary. A hard man when events demand it. Dedicated to his work and outstandingly brilliant as a hydro-geologist. Have you got the picture?'

She nodded.

Mr Lawson said very slowly and meaningly, 'You know, Mardie, if *I* had a daughter I would like to see her marry such a man.'

'Marry? But what has that to do with me? I mean . . .'

There was a long silence as he looked straight at her. Right into her eyes.

'That is a matter I thought you had a right to know – in advance. I'm reasonably sure – from a long experience of mankind – that Jard Hunter would like to ask you to marry him, Mardie. I know him well. I know he will come in here and ask you that question. He's a brief-and-to-the-point kind of man, Mardie. I imagine there'll be no preliminaries. No awkward sentimental declarations. At least these last are a matter of my opinion only.'

'But . . .' She was utterly bewildered.

'Please let me finish. I have heard there may have been some kind of attachment to that girl out at the Dig-in. Miss Seddon. Jard . . . being the kind of man he is . . . gave me no explanation whether that attachment had come to an end, nor at whose wish. How deep the attachment is or was – if ever – I cannot surmise. I'm a legal man and deal in facts, not suppositions. But he did tell me why he wished to propose marriage to you. He felt that I – as your trustee – was entitled to know. I think he is too chivalrous to give *you* the reasons. However, I think . . . because I have a special relationship with you . . . that you have a right to know those reasons. And not make a mistake because of "chivalry" alone. I want the best for you, Mardie, which means I want happiness for you.'

'Please go on.' Mardie's voice was very quiet. Her face had gone white.

'Remember what I said earlier. If I had a daughter I would like to see her marry such a man. I would go further now. I would like to see *you* marry Jard Hunter, Mardie. It would give great satisfaction and great happiness to me. But only *provided you knew what you were doing. And why.* And that you cared for the man.'

'Please go on.' Mardie had never fainted in her life, and she didn't think she was likely to faint now. But she felt strange, odd, as if she wasn't here. Or she'd been hit on the head or something.

'Well, here goes! I'm afraid an ugly rumour has been the rounds concerning that night of the crash. You may prefer to disregard it and let it die – if such things ever do die in an area that has a limited population.'

Mardie was calm now. In spite of the heat she was stone cold inside herself.

'You mean,' she said after a long pause, 'that because of what those two exploration-spy men said, my good name is being smeared – or something? That's how they put it in melodramatic terms, isn't it? You want me to know – because of your sense of justice to us both, Jard and me – that he will come and *offer to marry me to clear my fair name*? Is that it? And all this out of chivalry?'

'Yes,' Mr Lawson said quietly. 'Some things in life are tough to take, Mardie. For all of us. This is one of the tough ones for you. If you accept Jard's offer of marriage, I know he will be a good husband. And that he'll work at making you happy. He's that kind of man. But you are entitled to know his reasons *why;* and to know what you are doing.'

'Yes.'

'I kept my own counsel about deciding to let you know the facts, Mardie.'

There was a long silence. Mardie looked at her hands. Then she looked up and met Mr Lawson's eyes.

'Yet you are *not* giving me advice, are you? You are not advising me what to say to Jard?'

'That is so. It is your decision. I only wanted to make sure that you knew the facts.'

Mardie was calm still.

'Lots of people have arranged marriages,' she said unexpectedly. 'And they work out. People learn to love one another *afterwards.* It is something to do with respect for one another, isn't it? And tolerance. I've read about that somewhere.'

Mr Lawson was watching her closely. He was surprised at her thoughtfulness. Also her calm.

'I would like to tell you something, Mr Lawson,' she said. 'Please listen carefully. It's a confession. What those two men said about that night was, *in part,* true. It had to be that way because of the cold. Jard was suffering from shock. Shivers – rigors – that sort of thing. I want *you* to know that, but Jard could not possibly know it. He was not conscious. Mister Falldown knows it and he read it as the right thing for me to have done. He *understood.* The ground temperature would have been almost freezing. Jard's face was white with sweat, yet he had those rigors. There was only one bush rug. I undid his shirt. I took off my top clothes and I lay close to him. I put my arms round him and my legs wrapped round him. To keep him warm. For no other reason whatever. Warmth is the correct treatment for shock, isn't it?'

She paused. Then added sadly, 'There weren't any options, were there? Not open to me, anyway. It was that – or let him die. Or so I feared. That's how I saw it – right or wrong.'

Mr Lawson put out his hand and caught Mardie's two hands.

'Then marry him, Mardie – if you have any feeling for him – and let that philosophy of respect and tolerance of yours work it out for you. That is, *if you want to do that.* But not otherwise.'

'Yes. I would do that, except for one thing. It would be admitting that there had been something between us that wasn't proper, wouldn't it? Also there *is* another girl, like you said. Joanna. That makes it different. How fair would it be to Joanna? How fair to Jard? It would be like having him on, like buying a bargain, wouldn't it? A price for a price?'

Mr Lawson shook his head.

'You are, of course, right,' he said. 'But you will have to live down something very unpleasant. That might take time.'

She met his eyes steadily.

'Would you please tell me exactly why Jard had to discuss this with you? Why did he necessarily have a conscience about telling you first?'

'Because he knows what you and I both know. What everyone in the district knows. I am not your guardian – you are twenty-one and in law your own mistress. But I *am* the trustee of an estate in which you are involved. If Jard married you, he possibly stood to gain, material-wise. He, too, is in a very ambiguous situation. He knows I'm the trustee. He is an honourable man and he felt I should know the whole story, and of the circumstances that have put you both in such an unfortunate situation.'

Mardie really laughed this time. It was not a happy laugh. A rueful one.

'The age of chivalry is not yet dead, in spite of the permissive society, is it?'

'Not with a great many people. Irrespective of that, he did the right thing. The Breakaway is pegged for minerals in the name of your estate. He has this knowledge because of his connection with the Dig-in Exploration Company. It could look as if he were making use of this knowledge by . . .'

'Ditching Joanna and marrying me? Poor Jard. He is in a fix, isn't he? Marry a girl to save her good name, and at the same time be on a good thing if they make a nickel strike through that girl's property.'

'Now you understand why I had to tell you.'

Mardie smiled. 'Please don't worry any more, Mr Lawson. I shall turn him down flat and tell the world I've done it. That will let him out on all counts, won't it? He can keep his honour in both worlds. And maybe . . .' she faltered.

'Yes?'

'Maybe keep Joanna too.' The expression on Mardie's face was determined.

'My dear, I'm sorry this had to happen to you.'

'Don't be sorry. I'll live the crash episode down. You know something, Mr Lawson? I know the Richies will never think ill of me. And I know Mister Falldown will love me for it. That's fine, because I love the old bushman too. Now it will be mutual, won't it? I'll always have *three* friends who'll believe in me.'

Mr Lawson patted her hand. 'Good girl, Mardie. I admire your courage,' he said. He stood up and picked up his brief-case. 'Now I must go. I have business with the Exploration Company's city manager and David Ashton. They're getting ready for a visitation from the Directors as a group. With your permission, I'm hiring The Breakaway's utility and going out to the Dig-in. I don't know how long I'll be. This mining matter is business and sometimes it is complicated. But may I have the honour of booking in the first of the units built in your new motel? That is, when I can make it.'

Mardie kissed his cheek. 'May we have the honour of recording you as our very first client? We have a new Registry book and if anyone else calls in we'll leave the top space for you as already booked in Number One unit. That's making history, isn't it? I'll persuade Mrs Richie to bring out her best bottle of Drambuie to celebrate the occasion when you do get back here.'

'Let's make it a good Australian vintage wine instead. After all, in spite of its fame and Mrs Richie's reverence for it, Drambuie is a liqueur. We'll need a long drink, won't we?'

'Yes. It shall be Houghton's White Burgundy. That's not only a first-prize winner, it's a wine from this State.'

Mr Lawson grinned. 'My . . . you're coming on, Mardie! When you first came up, you didn't know the difference between an orange drink and a Porphery Pearl. Now you're on your way to putting down a cellar and becoming a connoisseur.'

'That'll be the day,' Mardie said gaily.

When he had gone she stopped playing at being gay. The very thought of Jard – with or without that night of the crash – made her heart turn over. He would come in and formally ask her to marry him, and she would have to say, 'Thank you very much, but I don't love you. I'm afraid the answer will have to be no.'

And Joanna would never know how good a friend she had in the mistress of The Breakaway Stop-over.

Not now . . . because some through-travellers had just pulled in . . . but later, in bed tonight, she would cry into her pillow.

Was there inside her a destiny always to be alone?

Mr Lawson had gone. The through-travellers had had tea, filled up with petrol and gone. A truck had pulled in and the men had had their drinks, bought cigarettes, a drum of oil because their engine was running a knock, swapped a little gossip with the Richies, then also gone on their way. Mrs Mansell had a chat about this and that over the Session when it came on. A white Mercedes Benz stopped while its owner asked for directions to the track leading off to the Dig-in.

'Take care,' Mrs Richie had advised. 'It's a bulldozed gravel track, and rough. Not surfaced as yet. Can be dangerous in places.'

The man had nodded.

'That's why I buy a Mercedes Benz and buy it white. It has all the safety devices built in and white's the only colour that can be seen clearly in any surroundings.'

Mrs Richie had looked disappointed. 'I thought it was because you were rich. A pretty dollar those cars cost when you have to pay import duty on top of a high price.'

The man had looked amused in a knowing kind of way, but he made no reply. It occurred to Mardie that this might be the city manager of the Dig-in Exploration Company who was to meet Mr Lawson out at the camp. In which case he probably *was* rich . . . but certainly wasn't saying so.

Her thoughts came back again to everyday reality. She must keep herself busy. The Breakaway was a wonderful place, she was thinking. One met the strangest people – people she would never have met in that suburban house in that suburban street of suburban houses, down south where her father and his new wife lived. She hoped they lived in happiness now they were no longer embarrassed by herself – the third person – which had made one person too many for a parental pair on honeymoon terms.

THIRTEEN

The white Mitchell cockatoos with their lovely yellow combs were flying overhead in masses. This meant the sun was westering and soon it would be sundown. The kangaroos, the brush-turkeys, the emus and even the lizards and snakes would be beating their pads to the water-hole a half-mile west of the bitumen. Then after sundown it would be night. Till then Mardie could not allow herself to stop smiling. She had to keep pretending gaiety and unconcern. That was good business and she and The Breakaway were 'in business'. Only when it was night and close-down time could she put her head on that pillow and have that little cry.

'Only a little one,' she promised herself. 'I do have to have that courage Mr Lawson mentioned. I need to steel it up for when Jard does come in. And asks that hundred-dollar question.'

If only she knew when.

She could at least do herself up a little for the occasion. Wash her hair, and brush it till it shone. Make the best of her make-up the way Joanna would have done. All as a matter of principle only, of course. She could even, accidentally, have put on one of her prettiest dresses.

After all, if the Spartans could comb their hair before they went into battle, she, Mardie Forrester, could dress herself up a little to be able to say 'no' to Jard Hunter. And mean it.

Mean it? Dear God up there – *I don't really want to be such an awful liar*!

Mardie did not do any of these things, for along with the bush animals coming with the evening to the water-hole, and about the time the western sky was a blazoned wall of red – when the mulga stood stiff and still against this sky like stick silhouettes – Jard Hunter came. And with him came Mister Falldown together with Dingo Pup. But before them came Joanna.

The brilliance had died out of the sky and everything over the spinifex and in the bush had gone silent. There was not the sound of a creep or a crawl, nor the whir of a bird's wings. Everything was still as if the world had not died but was standing quiet, motionless. It was the time of that statuesque silence of sundown in Australia. It was then Joanna came in the runabout from the Dig-in.

'Hallo, Mardie!' she said, walking straight into the office. She had left that whirligig hat of hers in the car so that Mardie knew this time she would not have to sit mesmerized by the twirling of a cotton-brimmed *Thing* on Joanna's forefinger.

'Hallo, Joanna. Nice to see you. Isn't it a wonderful evening?'

'Yes. It's exactly the same as any evening outback. The world stops. That is, except for me,' Joanna replied.

'Do please sit down and don't look as if something is bothering you. Shall I put on the tea jug or would you rather a drink in the sitting-room?'

'Neither for the moment,' Joanna said, sitting down in the chair angled by the windows so that whoever sat in it could see any comers from the outside world. She took out a cigarette and lit up.

'This is not a business call on the store, nor exactly a social call.' Joanna caught Mardie's eyes. 'Unless you like to turn it into that after I've said what I've come to say.'

'Well, let's hope,' Mardie said steadily. 'What is it you want to say, Joanna?'

'It's like this. I have a reputation for being blunt so please don't mind if I'm just that. Here goes. What's on with you and Jard? Half the outback's talking about you. David Ashton's been making as if he has a special claim on you, Mardie. I thought that was where your natural interest would be.'

And you've been talking and wondering too, Mardie thought, but not without a certain amount of sympathy.

'I like David,' she said, looking directly at Joanna. 'Perhaps we could become good friends. Who knows? There's nothing else to it but some word-flirtation over the radio – as yet. All the same . . .'

'Yes?'

'All the same, what has it to do with people talking?'

'Don't play Dumb-Dora with me, Mardie. You're sweet, unsophisticated and girlish. I suppose that's a pretty way of saying you do have something – and I like you for it. But you're not dumb. You couldn't have gone ahead with all this building round The Breakaway unless you had *some* brains.'

Mardie really smiled this time. 'Thank you, Joanna. Do you know something? I'm the one who's always been just that bit nervous of *your* brains.'

'It's not my brains that make me. It's temperament, determination and drive. That's what I have, Mardie. Drive. I'll be honest. I like to get my own way, too, so I set about whatever I'm doing or wanting and *get my own way.*'

'Good for you. But what is this all about, Joanna?'

'The 'copter crash. And the aftermath. That's what the outback's talking about. And I want you to do something to put a stop to it. For Jard's sake – if for no one else's.'

Not for my sake, Mardie thought. Everyone's concerned for Jard. Except Jard.

'How could I go about doing that?' she asked quietly.

'For one thing, you must know what it's all about. Everyone north or south of Twenty-six knows The Breakaway is like any other stop-over. It's a gossip exchange. So . . . they're making something of the fact that you and Jard weren't found after that 'copter crash till the following morning, as we all know. *But,* then found by a couple of baddies who happened to have a grievance against Jard. Which is where you come into it, of course.'

'Of course. I agree. I was there.'

'Exactly. Well, what I suggest to you is this. Pick on a couple you don't happen to like round the station fraternity. They could be roustabouts, stockmen, even a jackeroo. But leave the station owners out. That wouldn't pay off. They have too much influence and power out here.'

'Pick on this unnamed couple – for what?' Mardie asked, puzzled.

'You have that solicitor friend of yours in the area just now. He's been out at the Dig-in preparing for a Company "Meeting on Location", if you know what that means. It's what happens sometimes when every Board Member wants first-hand knowledge of what's going on. Lawson. Mr Lawson is the name. He's trustee for your estate, isn't he? That's common knowledge too.'

'Is there anything that isn't common knowledge?' Mardie asked, bewildered.

'Nothing of anything newsworthy, that's for certain,' Joanna said drily. 'Look, I think you can put that hot water jug on the boil, after all. I have a sudden hankering for tea.'

'Of course.' Mardie moved over to the side table and began the ritual of filling the electric jug with water, plugging it into the socket and switching on the current.

'You haven't explained everything,' she said, her back

still turned. 'Why should I pick on one or two roustabouts, etc.? Also what's Mr Lawson – my trustee or not – got to do with this roustabout-picking? Or would you advise . . .?'

'I wouldn't advise *anything*,' Joanna said bluntly, 'except I like you and I think you happen to need help in a sticky situation. It's simple. What you need to do for your own good is this. Get your friend, Mr Lawson, in here before he goes south again, and instruct him to clap a couple of writs for libel – or slander – whichever, on any two nobodies you don't happen to care for, and who happen to work around the stations or out with the prospectors.'

Mardie turned and stared at Joanna. She was astonished. '*Writs*? But why?'

'It will shut everyone else up, that's why. Mardie, you're not a fool. A writ out against one person, let alone two, will scare the daylights out of everyone else. You can always withdraw it later. It's the only way to clamp down the gossip.'

'The gossip being that the 'copter came down at sundown. And we weren't found till sun-up the next day?'

'That – and what's been added to it.'

Mardie had made the tea and now brought it to the table.

'Sugar? Biscuits?'

'No, thanks. I'm thirsty only.'

'And good at advice.' Mardie smiled, determined to be friendly. Joanna was, after all, only fighting for her own. Jard was her own. And she had a right to fight for him. She herself had no rights except to her own heart which would keep on doing a turnover even at the mere mention of his name.

They might have sipped their tea in silence except that . . . more than usual . . . one truck after another thundered along the bitumen. Two of them stopped under the trees and the drivers with their mates went into The Breakaway where Mr Richie was doing duty behind the store counter.

'I never knew such traffic,' Mardie said lightly. 'It could be People's Day at the Royal Show and the pop singers at Parkerville, all thrown on in one . . .' She broke off. There was the sound of another smaller vehicle, a utility, coming down the gravel cross-track to the bitumen. It could come from only one place. The back-track from the old abandoned gold mines out past Mister Falldown's shack. It was not Mister Falldown's day for coming in for stores. Neither did Mister Falldown drive a utility.

Joanna had lifted her head sharply, listening.

'That's one of the Dig-in's utes,' she said.

'But coming from the wrong direction. How could you possibly know that?' Mardie was wondering at Joanna's skills again. Not doubting her. There seemed nothing with which Joanna was not accurately acquainted, either in matters of good judgment or technical know-how.

'It's missing on one cylinder. That's how I know. And it's Jard driving. Don't ask me how I know *that,* Mardie. I don't have second sight or second hearing. Jard went out to see Mister Falldown, and *not* to see his menagerie. It's about that water seepage below the north mesa range. Old Mister is Jard's guide, philosopher and friend when it comes to the ancient tribal water-holes. Below the mesa those water-holes form a link which means there's a pattern to the underground lake out there. Artesian well, if you prefer to call it that.'

Joanna had become the geologist again.

'I suppose that underground lake could be as big as the sea?' Mardie asked tentatively. Anything rather than be concerned that it was *now* Jard Hunter had come . . . not tomorrow or next week. *Now*, Joanna was here so the name of the game would never be 'competition' as far as she, Mardie, was concerned.

Why worry? What with Joanna's presence, those truckies in the store, and possibly Mister Falldown, there'd be no formal proposal of marriage this early evening. Nor . . . alas . . . any formal rejection of that chivalrous gesture.

What she wanted of life was companionship and love. Not a way of life that was only a status symbol.

'As big as the Caspian by Jard's mapping so far,' Joanna was saying crisply. 'But there's more. The information needed is – does it all link up? Is it moving water? In other words an underground *river*! If so, it would give mining in this area as big a fillip as a major nickel strike.'

She had pushed her empty cup and saucer aside. She stood up, stretched as if taking in strength and air for important sorties about to take place.

'I think I'll go and see what they want,' she said, moving towards the door. 'Thanks for the tea, Mardie.' This last sounded like a dismissal . . . which was odd because it was Joanna who was leaving the room. Not Mardie.

Mardie turned to her accounts with only half her heart on the job.

The ute with a miss in one cylinder had come to a stop under the trees along the side boundary. Mardie tried not to glance up through the window but Will Power wasn't with her this evening. She saw the drive door swing open and his lean shadowy figure emerge from the car. Mister Falldown must have left the far side of the car at the same time, because they came together across the gravel to the cement walk, then past the trellis. The luminous purple shades of evening were darkening the western sky but his figure was unmistakable. And the way he walked. That quiet yet determined tread. Mister Falldown was a darker, sturdier figure. He walked less quickly, so followed Jard on to the cement path.

Mardie bent her head over the table and put her hands over her eyes.

Why did this have to happen to her?

What else could she have done that night? Deep in her heart she knew it was a glad thing to do. Not just a duty. She had fallen for him long-time before that 'copter ride. Let alone that 'copter crash.

Mrs Richie came across from the store to Mardie's office.

'Aren't you going to change for dinner, dear?' she asked. 'We've visitors. The best kind.'

'I know Joanna came in to see me before she went along to the store.'

'But Jard's here too. He asked where you were, and were you too busy to be interrupted, even for dinner.' She looked at Mardie with an odd yet kindly expression on her face. 'Even for *him*?' she added gently.

You too! Mardie thought. So this is what gossip does even to one's best friends.

Mardie added a little sauce to Will Power this time. 'Not for dinner because I'm not hungry. And not *specially* for Jard. But there's Mister Falldown too. I'm not too busy for Mr Falldown – *ever*.'

Mrs Richie thought hard, and decided the least said the better. 'Well, we'll be ready as soon as you like, dear.'

By the time Mardie, polished up but not overdoing it, arrived in the sitting-room, Joanna was on the point of departure. She didn't look exactly pleased but wore her most professional scientific front.

'Sometimes one wishes the Company could manage without a Board of Directors bent on interfering with what we are doing,' she was saying to Jard, who was walking with her to the door. 'After all, *we* are the professionals and there's hardly one of them will understand the assays or what they mean.'

'But they do pay our salaries,' Jard said with his usual half-smile. 'Yours is a whopper, Jo. For that alone you have to go back, never mind whether they can read your maps or interpret your assays, or not.'

If he noticed Mardie come in, he gave no sign yet. He was busy holding Joanna's arm, calling her 'Jo' and placating her with a more than kindly firmness. 'Sorry to have brought such a stinker message,' he added. 'I'm afraid you'll have to go. Remember the shareholders are sitting on the Directors' backs too, and the Stock Market is poised at the ready.'

He took Joanna out to her runabout. He was not away so markedly long. Mardie surmised that that short farewell could be because Joanna's presence at the Dig-in was required urgently. Why had she herself looked at her watch? Because she couldn't help it, of course!

Jard came just as Mardie was trying to persuade Mister Falldown to stay the night with them at The Breakaway.

'You have no chance of winning that plea, Mardie,' Jard said quietly. 'Mister never sleeps anywhere but on his own patch. Or in the bush.'

Mardie's eyes caught his, and suddenly she felt panic. There was something more than kindly in his expression. There was a sort-of *message*. She wasn't imagining it. It was a you-and-me one.

'You look well,' she said. 'Perhaps getting a bump on the head does you good.'

'Giving my brains a shake up undoubtedly did me good,' he said, smiling. 'I'm sorry I involved you too, Mardie.'

Damn that smile, Mardie thought wildly. If only he'd go back to being the mystery man. A shadow and no more!

'Life is a chain of adventures, isn't it?' she said with a smile. 'That was one more adventure for me to chalk up and think about in my old age.'

'Old age!' Mrs Richie interrupted indignantly. 'A young girl like you thinking about such a thing!' she said. 'Now if you will please let Mr Richie pour you both a drink, then come and eat my dinner before it's ruined. And talk about "young age". That's all Mr Richie and I think about. We get younger every day.'

Mardie loved the way the Richies always referred to one

another as Mr and Mrs. It gave them a sort-of old-fashioned dignity. Some of it spilled off on other people, particularly the customers who were not always so easy to handle.

They had their drinks and later dinner. They talked of incidental things like the fact that one could grow bananas along the Gascoyne River because this river flowed underground during the Dry, at a time when the surface river-bed was as barren as a bone. And why a sunset at Bali, more than a thousand miles northward, could produce a sunset as far south as the Swan River, the glory of which was indescribable.

Later, when Mrs Richie had insisted she would take the dishes out and attend to them whether Mardie liked it or not, and when Mr Richie had departed to close up the store for the evening, Mardie was left with only Mister Falldown and Jard. She said a little prayer that Mister would, for once, stay put. But this was not to be so. He was going back to his solitary home in the bush – walking. And *now*.

'But you can't do that.' Mardie pleaded. 'Not tonight. I'm sure Jard will drive you back.'

'Mister Falldown always walks,' he said of himself in his soft, rather thick voice. 'This fella only ride when Jard say "Mister you come, I need you". But he never say "Mister you *go*". So I go *my way,* Miss Mardie, if you'll 'scuse me. Jard knows. I always go my way.'

'He does, Mardie,' Jard said quietly. 'But first I want him to tell you why I did say "Mister you come, I need you" today. Go ahead, Mister.'

The old bushman looked at Mardie with his dark, gentle eyes. A silly thing to think – but they were almost loving eyes.

'Jard tell me to come because I found you when that sky 'copter fell down in the bush like one time I fall down on my head and forget who I am.'

Mardie's heart kept missing a beat now because she knew this was the Big Moment, and what this conversation would be about.

'Yes. You did indeed,' she said. 'Thank God for that, Mister Falldown. Do you believe in God?'

'I believe in some Fella must be Boss out there in Dreamtime country – maybe. But I forget what my father told me. So I just believe. No more talk about this one thing.'

'Well . . . it must be some Fella out there in Dreamtime country who sent you to find us,' Mardie said gently. 'So I thank Him for that as well as you.'

She did not look at Jard. She didn't want to know what he was thinking. Specially she didn't want to know what he was looking like just now. She wanted him to be the mystery-man-stranger all over again. Nothing more.

'Tell us both what you saw when you found us, Mister,' Jard said. Very quiet. Very firm.

'I saw you all-about dead fella, Jard. And Missy looking after you like a good wife looks after her right man.'

'Did she *mind* looking after me like a . . .' He paused, then added with a whimsical smile . . . 'a good wife?'

'No. No. She was all cut-up sad because you were hurt. She wanted you better quick but she didn't know for sure she'd bin doing right thing okay.'

'And had she?'

'Everything right way all the time. She had sense, this one. That other one, Jo – she got granite in her head. Plenty rich granite. Hard stuff that rock. Maybe lots of nickel too, and that other stuff – all stone.'

'Thank you both for this cross examination of the case of the crashed 'copter . . .' Mardie said as lightly as she could. She, too, had to make it a case. Put, and defended. After all, the bush telegraph had been the same thing as the prosecution. She wished she could think of a joke or a witty crack . . . the way David Ashton would have done. It could have turned this discussion into entertainment only. Then finish.

The thought of David Ashton, his jokes and his wise-cracks, his kindness and his gentle flattery over the air, softened the lump that was becoming unbearably hard in her breast. Perhaps if David liked her, the way Joanna insisted he did, she could marry *him* and live happy ever after. That is – if he ever asked her.

But alas! All that was a day-dream too!

Mister Falldown had gone. And gone *his* way. Walking.

'Come outside and look at the night sky, Mardie,' Jard said. 'I feel like walking. Mrs Richie's cooking is too good. It needs to be digested slowly to be appreciated.'

He stood up and held out his hand – more as an invitation than possibly expecting Mardie to put her hand in his.

Better get it all over and done with, she thought. The Richies always withdrew to their own private section after they closed down The Breakaway. They probably would not notice the fact that she and Jard had gone to spend half an hour under the blue-black sky, the so-brilliant stars, and the first gold haze of a moon that was already rising in the east.

She put her hand lightly in his, then as lightly withdrew it as they moved away.

'It would be rather pleasant,' she said. 'Where shall we walk? Round The Breakaway or along the bitumen?'

'Neither. The gravel track out westwards could be a change. Willing?'

'Yes, of course.'

FOURTEEN

Jard was looking at her; she could feel his eyes on her. The moonlight would be lighting *her* face as it lit his.

It was no good dreaming dreams. He only had to look at her like that and she was like snow fallen on warm ground, and was melting. All this only in the name of *chivalry*! Grand but sad.

'Why didn't you bring David Ashton with you, Jard?' she said at last. It was something to say to break the silence.

'Why should I bring him? In any case he's bogged down with a visiting team of Directors about to appear at the Dig-in. They're arriving by plane.'

'Perhaps he couldn't come. But if he had come, he would help me. That's why. You see, Jard, I know what this is all about. This talk now, and why you brought Mister Falldown in. You wanted to prove to me that you trusted me and that you knew that all that happened that night was the right thing to have happened. Then you wanted to make some recompense for any – well – sort-of complications I might have suffered. If David had come I would have someone to help *me* just as you have brought Mister Falldown to help *you* – I mean in this attempt at, well, *reparation* for crashing me down in the bush in that 'copter of yours.'

'*Mardie . . .*'

She lifted her head and mustered dignity as her help-all this time. And forgot about Will Power.

'Why don't you offer me fifty dollars for my nursing services – amateurish though they were – and settle the account that way? That is what you want to do, isn't it, Jard? Settle an account?'

She smiled, so as to turn this matter into an affair of inconsequential chit-chat. Something of no importance. If David had been here he would have triggered off her own minor ability to make funnies with childish jokes and riddles. That was David's talent. He could turn anything into a laugh. And she could and would have responded.

Jard was being thoughtful. He was seeing Mardie's plea for David in a different light.

'You and he – that is David – are good friends, aren't you, Mardie?' he asked quietly.

'Yes. We do our courting over the air so it's not very private, I'm afraid.'

'*Courting*? Are you serious?'

'Of course.'

'You mean there is something *serious* between you and David? Are you in love with him, Mardie?'

'If friendship is love, then I suppose you could say I love him.' Mardie was being light and airy about the whole thing. 'Don't you think laughter is a wonderful thing, Jard? If you love laughter you love the person who makes it. Do I sound a bit screwy, or is my logic *real* logic to you?'

Jard did not answer at once.

'It's more than logic,' he said at length. 'I think it's telling me something. But not all.'

Mardie laughed . . . again it was the tiniest bit forced but she was not aware of this.

'It's all you need to know,' she said. 'Please don't ask me any more.' She was getting herself tangled up in this game of words and was beginning not to understand what she was saying . . . or even wanting to say it. She just didn't know how to prevent Jard making that chivalrous declaration that Mr Lawson had warned her about. She would have to say 'No', and that might ruin any friendship she would like, and *wanted*, to have with Jard.

'Such a pity!' he said unexpectedly.

'A pity?' Mardie asked in surprise.

'Yes. You see I'd like to be a little in love with you myself. But I'm not quite sure which kind of love is specifically allocated to one's ability to make laughter.'

'You mean like some people love to make a pudding?'

'No. I mean like Making Love. Capital letters.'

Here we are all tangled up in words again, Mardie thought.

Neither of us can say what we really mean.

The only thing she could do was keep it up, till it was time to turn about and go indoors.

'I've been in love with laughter all my life,' she said lightly. 'Though it was in short supply – a bit – before I came up here. Then David made me laugh again. You see . . . I lost my mother . . .'

'Yes, I know. Mrs Richie told me about it before you came to The Breakaway.'

'And you sympathize? Yes . . . well . . . thank you very much. Jard. Have you ever loved someone *very much*? Oh dear! I didn't mean to put it that way. But you are probably in love with someone already. I mean – it's only natural . . .'

He glanced at her but she did not see it and did not see the expression in his eyes.

'Of course . . .' she went on hurriedly. By now she was beyond extricating herself from this silly word-game. 'It would have to be someone with the same interests that you have, wouldn't it?' she went on, afraid her voice was getting scratchy. 'I mean sort-of scientific. Exploration. All those things . . .'

'That was what I used to think myself. But then I saw a vision. Have you ever seen a vision, Mardie? Or don't you believe in such things?'

'What sort of a vision? A wonderful stream of underground water that would make a mine possible?'

'True in a way. If they – the Company – decide a mine is possible out at the Dig-in their greatest asset would be access to permanent water. But that wasn't the vision I was talking about.'

'Am I allowed to ask?'

'It was a face. A girl's face. Lovely, soft, luminous. Dark eyes that had a light in them. And kindness. I only saw that face for so short a while. Then it was gone.'

'You mean you fell in love with a *face*?' Mardie asked, incredulous. 'The rest of it might have been hump-backed and bow-legged.'

'But it wasn't,' he said ever so gently.

'How do you know if you only saw the face?' She was quite bewildered. Jard, the strong, silent mystery man turning out to be a dreamer of dreams? She thought only girls were like that.

'I do know. The big trouble is, I don't quite know how to go about courting the owner of that face. I'm not exactly accustomed to . . . well . . . to making advances to young ladies. Can you give me some advice?'

'If it were me I would make her laugh,' Mardie suggested. 'Everybody loves a smiler . . .' She broke off. A new thought struck her. It was like the beat of that spread-eagled wing one moment before the 'copter was hit. *Then it couldn't be Joanna, after all*! Joanna had her brilliance and her efficiency. But real laughter? Well, some. A smiler anyway – when it suited her. And she made no bones about being ready and waiting for Jard. She didn't need *courting*. Jard must surely know *that*.

'I've been too busy and too serious about my work too long,' he was saying. 'I often have a good laugh myself but I'm not David. I don't have the gift of making other people laugh.'

'Not yet.'

'Not yet?'

'It's easy . . . if you read the Children's Page in the *Sunday Independent*. They have a special column for jokes sent in by the children.'

'You think that's where David gets his jokes?'

'Well . . . some of them.'

'So you read them too?'

'Some of them.'

'Then I'll take your advice. Get The Breakaway store to order the journal for me, will you?'

Mardie really laughed this time.

'Oh, Jard,' she said, 'you really are funny. There! You've made me laugh. You see? It's easy. You're on the way to being a funny man already.'

He was silent for almost a minute. Then he took Mardie's arm, but he said nothing. He knew how to draw into the background. How to listen. But what was he actually thinking?

She longed to hug his hand to her, where it rested in the bend of her elbow, but dared not. If it had been David she was sure it would have been easy. Different. It wouldn't have meant anything but fun-making and friendship. With Jard it would almost mean violation of that deep inner reserve that was part of his make-up.

The moon had risen now. She didn't dare look away from him, nor quite at him.

'What are you thinking, Mardie?'

'Thinking? Why, I don't think I really know . . .'

She could not tell him about all those awkward sorrows

that touched a girl's heart when she knew, or feared, she had fallen in love with someone. And for no very good reason except that once she had held him and cradled him as if he were then – at the time – a wounded child. And one who cares for a wounded child loves that child. This because, for that little while, it *belongs*.

Yet Jard was a man. Infinitely higher up in the world of affairs than she was herself.

In the daylight, striding across that tarmac, whirling the ute in under the trees by The Breakaway, quietly talking within the walls of that same Breakaway . . . or even nurssing an old bushman's dingo pup . . . there was something *superior* about him. His eyes were kind but aloof. They reasoned with one – though gently. They were far away. High up.

How could she dare to think of him as one would think of a wounded child!

In the bright moonlight his eyes took her in. What did he think he saw? What would those eyes look like if he fell in love?

Ah! But he had said he had fallen in love . . . *with a face.* Does a man marry someone just because she has the right kind of face?

'I think we'd better go back now, don't you?' she said, so quietly her voice didn't sound like her own at all. It might be safer to insist on going back. Then he would have lost all opportunity to put that fateful question.

She had to ward him off somehow!

'I wanted to ask you something,' he said as they turned, retracing their footsteps. Mardie's heart nearly stopped stone dead. It was coming after all – that question.

'Yes?'

'Would you let me take you out to see the Dig-in? From the ground view this time. We could go in the ute if you don't mind a rough trip. It's a bulldozed track only – gravel for about half the distance. I could show you then where we could bring the water through for a temporary period. Enough to set up for diamond drilling along the strike line they've already tested. That is, *if* the Company Directors are satisfied with Joanna's assays. They'll have seen the cuttings we've brought up from the percussion drilling. They'll take at least two lots back with them to Company headquarters – all packed in neat little plastic bags.'

'Is that why the Directors are arriving? Not just to hold a

"Meeting-on-Location"?'

'In effect they will have had a "Meeting on Location". That will be to decide whether or not diamond drilling is justified. And to take possession of the relevant cuttings. These days Directors have to be doubly careful before they make their reports public. There's been a few misleading statements made by other Companies in the past. Hence the blow-up on the Stock Markets. Senate Inquiry Committees and all that. Many burned fingers, I'm afraid.'

'Yes . . . I've sort-of read the headlines. I'm afraid I don't understand it very much.'

She could see there was something whimsical about his smile.

'But you'd like to understand more?' he asked.

'Oh . . . only because I live here. It's my territory, isn't it? I don't want information like those exploration spies . . .' she broke off. Inadvertently she'd brought herself back to that one dangerous topic. The baddies who had come, gone, and spread nasty rumours.

This time he really laughed. And it was a glorious sound. He wasn't up-tight any more.

'I must explain,' he said. 'I want to make amends for spoiling our last excursion out into the Never, when that blasted 'copter crashed. I want to take you out safely this time – four wheels on the ground – and show you the Exploration camp at ground level.' His eyes were watching her and for once she had the idiotic idea there was a touch of mischief in them.

'That way I won't have to pay you fifty dollars for your nursing services, will I?' he added.

'Now you're teasing me. You know I didn't really mean that.'

'Of course I knew it. But . . . you're really smiling now. I'm beginning to make the grade at getting acquainted with laughter after all. Who knows? I might catch up with David in your esteem.'

Mardie was so surprised she was silent. Jard – almost hearing the silence – lost his smile.

'That is, unless David is destined always to have priority in matters of laughter. Am I right, Mardie? Is it David who will always come first in your category of the male being who is the number one entertainer?'

She knew there was a serious query beyond his surface words. In one way it alarmed her.

'Please, please, Jard! Don't tell David I've been talking about him this way, will you? He might think . . .'

'Yes? Think what?'

'Well . . . I don't want to embarrass him.'

'I shan't tell him anything, Mardie. But apart from that, I've not known David to be serious about anything on earth except how much and to what value there is nickel under that ground out there at the Dig-in. I could, of course, throw in his urgent need of constant and plentiful water available somewhere within the immediate environment. That is, *if* the Directors decide to go ahead with the diamond drilling. That could ultimately lead to creating a mine. And that's what exploration is all about.'

Somehow, almost without noticing it, they were back at The Breakaway.

Jard held out his hand to say good night. She put her hand in his. It was a hard, strong hand and it held hers firmly. He looked straight into her eyes.

'Thank you for a lovely evening,' he said gently. 'And thank you for being you, Mardie . . . specially for that night after the 'copter crash. And, you will let me take you out to the Dig-in? They're putting on a film show for the workers and the station people round about. They're all coming. It will be quite a party, and I think you'll enjoy it.'

'Thank you for asking me. Yes, I'll come. With pleasure.' Her hand was still in his. He was still holding it, almost as if meaning to keep it.

'Good,' he said at length. 'I'll let David know. He'll be delighted, I'm sure.'

He dropped her hand and turned away as if to cross the gravel to his ute. Mardie stood fixed to the spot.

With that talk about David I've put him off the question about marriage, she thought. But poor David. What have I done to him? There's still that ugly rumour. Even if David liked me – in that certain way – he'd be the one stuck with spots tarnishing a once 'fair name', wouldn't he? I can almost hear them already – 'That girl! How many men does she sleep with before she gets to the altar?'

She watched the tall shadowy figure cross the gravel and open the ute's front drive door. She heard the engine start up and the odd irregular miss of one cylinder not firing. She watched him swing the ute round, throw up gravel and dust, then speed out through The Breakaway's drive-in then on to the bitumen. For minutes afterward she heard the sound of his going, growing fainter and fainter. Then fading out to silence.

It was like listening to Love . . . Going, going, *gone*!

She'd managed it all herself. She had saved him from having to appease his honour by herself refusing to salvage her own. All by the gentle art of misrepresentation. She had misrepresented, very subtly she hoped, her feelings for David. *Joanna, here I come! I'm not as clever as you about scientific matters, but I'm just as clever, if not more so, about handling difficult situations. Even if I had to do it at poor darling David's expense.*

As she turned and went into The Breakaway she didn't feel proud of her so-clever achievement. She wanted to reach for her pillow – and *cry into it.*

The next morning David came over the air to Mardie in her office.

'Red Wine to Bickleys Brandy. Come in, if you're there.'

'Bickleys Brandy. I'm here, David. How are you all getting on with your Board of Directors? I believe they've all arrived. Did you give them a good breakfast? Mrs Richie insists that a good breakfast puts everyone in a good mood for the day.'

'You bet we did. And at the Company's expense – which they probably noted. However, Joanna kept the peace. She's a wizard at playing political chess when the game's on.'

'It wouldn't be good politics always to beat the Directors at the game, would it?'

'No. That's where her brilliance comes in. She loses on purpose. So that's a win, isn't it?'

'Oh David, I think you're having me on again! What can The Breakaway do for the Dig-in today? Get another load of stores ready?'

'You have your miserable penny-pinching mind on commerce again, sweetheart. Just forget The Breakaway for once and think of a few breaking hearts out here on the flat of the spinifex desert. We're in need of you. Badly.'

'Badly? I can't believe it. But, David dear . . . if you-all out there need me I'm at the ready. What can I do for you?'

'Like I said. Come out here and be seen. Jard said you'd come out for the film show – if he brought you.'

'Did he put that proviso on it – that *he* was to bring me?'

'He did.'

'Why?'

'I don't know. I thought you'd tell me.'

'I'd tell you everything you wanted to know, David dear, so long as I knew the answer to give.'

'That means you've already cooked it up with him, hey?'

'It means he invited me. And he said he'd take me out there. And I said, "Thank you very much I'd like to go".'

'Ho hum! So that cuts me out, doesn't it?' David's voice pretended to be doleful.

'It means he asked me first, David darling, that's all. When is it?'

'Wednesday. Too late for you to buy a new dress, but wear your prettiest, won't you? I want to show you off.'

'Whatever for? I mean to whom, and why?'

'I'll tell you when I see you. I've a special *Special* waiting for you, darl. It's a personal question so I can't ask it over the air. There just might be someone who can cut in on our wave length. Bring the Richies, won't you? Over and out, sweetie.'

'You're full of mystery this morning, David. But I'll be there wearing my very best. 'Bye for now. Over and out.'

Mardie hitched the speaker to its hook and sat looking at the two-way in silence.

What did he mean?

She had a sudden feeling of terror. Jard hadn't been dropping David hints that she, Mardie, was head over heels in love with him? Dear heaven! She had indeed scrambled the omelette in giving Jard a cause *not* to ask her that certain question. Had she gone too far and made a mud mixture instead?

She sat and worried. Then had a bright idea.

She could be going – right up to the last minute. Then be ill. The only sort of illness one could collect at short notice was a headache. And didn't a 'headache' sound too weak an excuse? Besides, she wanted to go. The Richies would want to go and if she said she had a headache, or any other ailment, one of them would insist on staying back and looking after her.

So go she must.

The decision made, Mardie felt better. In fact she began to feel happy, and this in spite of her guilty feeling. She wanted to see the Dig-in at ground level. She wanted to wear her nicest dress and be gay and have fun. She would go, and she would just have to keep her wits about her as she had when she'd taken that walk with Jard. Then somehow – like Joanna playing political chess – ward them both off. David and Jard. Jard and David.

Suddenly she felt sad again.

Wasn't it a wonderful thing to have two men . . . two marvellous men . . . wanting you for their girl friend? One of them only thinking he *ought* to propose marriage, though for the wrong reasons entirely. The other perhaps pretending just for the fun of this week's latest joke.

But it was wonderful all the same, for whatever motive.

Lots of girls had no one at all. She hadn't had anyone at home. Because of her mother's long illness she had had to rush home straight from work. Her father worked back at night so often she could rarely go out at night herself. She had lost all contacts during that tragic time.

But now she had two nice people who wanted to be kind and friendly, as with David. Kind and honourable, as with Jard.

She wasn't alone any more. That old, old adage – 'Better to have loved and lost than never to have loved at all'. It wouldn't be a case of having 'lost' with Jard. Honesty had won. That was quite something to mark up for herself.

Ah well!

FIFTEEN

The day for the visit to the Dig-in came.

Mardie began to feel excited. The prospect of seeing a mining exploration camp at work lifted her spirits. She almost forgot to think about her relationships with David and Jard. She feared her present plight might be bordering on the ridiculous: so best try and forget it. Easier said than done, most of the time. She knew that night of the 'copter crash had not been something ridiculous. It had been something that would stay with her for ever. So was important. She just wanted to stop being hurt by it. If only she knew *how*!

You could love a hundred people, she reasoned. But ever only be in love with one. Well, maybe.

Now here was something coming that could be one more adventure – and even be *fun*. A trip to the Dig-in *ground* level.

The furniture experts had departed from the motel units and until their wares ultimately arrived and were set in place each in its own home, the units were closed up. However Number One, the king-suite, had been 'booked' for Mr Lawson and the firm's specimen furniture installed in it. He had had to return south unexpectedly and had been flown from the Dig-in in a Company plane. He was expected back shortly and had promised Mardie he would call in at The Breakaway first in order to be the first to inhabit that *special* suite.

Mr Richie refused point blank to leave The Breakaway for the whole day and evening outing to the Dig-in. He could not be budged.

'Never since The Breakaway was first built has it been closed to night callers,' he said flatly. 'All anyone ever has to do to open us up is ring the bell, and that fact is known from the top end of the State to the Southern Ocean. I'll not risk it to any stand-in who might stuff cotton wool in his ears before he falls asleep come sundown.'

'But – '

'As for the daytime hours! Well, yes. I can find a stand-in all right. I'll borrow someone from the pub at Pindarra. I'll need that and we can give him double pay. You agree, Mardie? We're all *three* partners in the store side of this property, aren't we?'

'By which you mean you have your vote on a decision not to close up even for one evening. And your dear darling wife would support you. Two to one against me, I can't win, can I? All right, darling Mr Richie, I give in without any vote being taken. But everyone will be sorry you won't be there for the barbecue. They'll miss you.'

'Sure. But they'll all come in here a week later to make up for it. Think of the business we'll do that day!'

Mardie laughed and called him a 'money-minded rogue'. Yet because Mr Richie was staying behind she felt proud. The Breakaway in its history had never been closed against a knock, or a push of the bell. It would live up to its reputation.

Jard came early in the morning. Not long after sun-up actually.

'You must have left before moon-down,' Mrs Richie said reprovingly. 'Man, you'll be worn out before the day's done. Not much fun in that for you.'

'I'll take *you* for a moonlight drive some time in the

small hours of the morning, Mrs Richie,' Jard said with a grin. 'That's when earth and heaven are at peace with one another. The best time of all. To see the false dawn . . .' He broke off.

What had crossed his mind? Mardie wondered. It had been false dawn when those two rifle-carrying baddies had come. And he, Jard, had opened his eyes and looked at her. Had he remembered?

Oh *no*! He had closed his eyes again. He had slipped back into semi-consciousness again – if he'd ever even reached that stage when he opened his eyes.

He couldn't possibly have known or recognized the fact of her partly unclad body holding him close to her. He just wasn't with it.

There was room for all three of them in the passenger seat of Jard's ute as they drove out shortly after nine o'clock.

'You sit in the middle, Mardie,' Jard had said, looking down at her. 'You're the smallest. We must give Mrs Richie plenty of room to fall out comfortably if the door-lock gives way.'

He was joking but his smile as he looked down at Mardie, now cushioned comfortably against his shoulder, seemed to hold something special in it. She wondered what? But then she was beyond ever interpreting the expressions in Jard's eyes. At first he had seemed such a reserved and silent man. She thought he was still that person, but events had thrown them together in a strange situation. Maybe the difference in him, and what she could read in his eyes, was due to some changes those events had brought about. From indifference to kindness? Yes, she thought, that was it!

They said little as they drove along. They had left the bitumen and were following a side track over a strip of bull-dozed clay-pan. Next they were crossing an upland desert of sand and gravel plain, ancient and ageless. It had been just this for millions of years. Age was a thing one could not define in figures, Mardie thought, not on the outback.

'They're the oldest land forms in Australia – those dips and mesa outposts,' Jard said when Mardie asked about them. 'This part of the continent has changed little since Pre-Cambrian times – that's a geological expression for saying six hundred million years or more.'

'As old as that?' Mardie was awed.

'The "undatable oddlands" we call them,' Jard said.

'Not so odd when they give up riches like gold and now nickel . . .'

'There aren't many places in the world that render up such odds,' Jard said with a wry grin. 'That gravel you see all over the flat lands is laterite. Broken down residue of denuded mountains. The mesas sticking up singly here and short ranges there are the last and hardest rock cores left from the weathering of the hardest and oldest rock forms of them all. The ultra-basics where the minerals are found in dykes.'

'And if we all lived for another few million years and left them untouched, they too would weather down to gravel rubble?'

'Laterite!' he corrected her mildly. 'Rubble indeed! Don't let David hear you say that! It's in the lateritic bands we first look for the sulphides. They indicate the possible presence of nickel underground. It's along those lateric gossans we use the rotary percussion drills, mostly called down-the-hole power drills, to look for dykes of pay dirt. If any. Do you know what pay dirt means, Mardie?'

'An area worked over that will pay with precious metals,' Mardie said almost glibly. 'I read that somewhere. I've been sending for books that will tell me accurately about this land I live in now. It's like reading a mystery story about the long, long ago. Mister's Dreamtime land.'

'I see you're getting the bug. You'll make a geologist yet.'

'But not like Joanna . . .' This time she spoke almost sadly. 'She went to University and really learned about it properly.'

'But not about human relations,' he said unexpectedly.

Now what did he mean by that? Mardie wondered. Perhaps it was something to do with Joanna's stark-type statements when she sometimes talked to other people. Perhaps not. Perhaps he meant Joanna did not show the right kind of affection for people close to her. Himself? Maybe this was why he himself had been strangely aloof and silent when she had first known him.

Supposing she herself became the greatest heroine of all time and be the one to tell him Joanna *cared.* What then?

Well, she wasn't heroine enough for that. She knew – intuitively – that Joanna's caring was really a matter of possessing and Jard was not the kind of man who would like being possessed. He wasn't a major specimen of highly valued nickel. Mardie, on that fateful crash night, had seen him helpless and in *need*, conscious or unconscious. She had seen and known him – very human. In those few precious hours when he had neared consciousness *he held her*, as she held him. Then he was at peace before he passed out again.

In the heart of every man a crying schoolboy?

She stared out over the brown spinifex land beyond the ironstone cappings across the broad drainage lines of shallow clay-pans, and the flat uplands between them; and thought about it. She knew more about Jard than Joanna would ever know. Yet this knowledge was something she had to keep locked in her heart. Perhaps . . . mercifully . . . some day she would forget. Time did pass, didn't it? Just as those denuding mesas and the wind-eroded dunes forming in shallow circular clay lakes now proved. Time – millions of years – had passed for them. But it *had* passed.

Well . . . she hoped she didn't have to live six million years to forget.

Mister Falldown remembered through generations of forefathers the mountains and rivers, the water lakes of his Dreamtime Land that once had been here, and which he now believed was out there . . . beyond space and other galaxies. Where the Big Fella ruled. Moon walks would mean nothing to Mister Falldown. He *knew* there was a land far far beyond a mere earth-tied moon!

'Why so quiet, Mardie?' Jard asked. 'You are having a very long "think", aren't you?'

'I was thinking about Mister Falldown and his Dreamtime Land.'

'For them – the Mister Falldowns – there is such a place.'

Mardie was surprised. 'Do you believe that?'

'I'm a geologist – on the hydro side – and I know something of their legends and the things they've passed on down the generations. Geologically speaking, what they know and describe must have happened before. What they remember through their rites, sacred totems and taboos, tallies with what *we* geologists do know happened long ages here on earth. Mister Falldown's limits of geography are far beyond our galaxy. Outer space and the moon are small fry to him. There are millions of galaxies that we can't even dream about. *They* do.'

He looked down at her and smiled. It was that glorious heart-warming smile she had glimpsed only once or twice before.

'You put so much store on laughter taking the first prize in life,' he said whimsically. 'I give equal prize to *wonder*.

That's the fascination of the outback, Mardie. Sheer wonder. Think of the age of these rock stones we're driving over. Pre-Cambrian. Six hundred million years at the minimum.'

'Yes,' she said slowly. 'It's like a sort-of magic. It takes a hold on one, doesn't it? I mean the wonder of it.'

'If you ask me,' said Mrs Richie in her prime state of matter-of-factness, 'I'd put more store on you watching where you're driving, Jard. Next minute you'll hit a pot-hole if you keep looking at Mardie. Then we'll have a broken axle on our hands. Goodbye big-fella party at the Dig-in!'

Jard laughed. 'You always were a one for a party, weren't you, Mrs Richie? If you can't go to one, you give one at The Breakaway. When's the next coming up?'

'I have it planned already but I'm not telling you when or why.'

'Oh ho! A mystery?'

'Not to me and Mr Richie. Though I'll admit it might be to you two, and a few more, for the time being.'

'We'll have to wait and see, won't we?'

Mrs Richie pursed her lips and nodded her head thoughtfully. 'I give it a month,' she said as if pronouncing matters for Judgment Day. 'Want to take a bet on it, Jard?'

He shook his head, watching the track carefully now, for they were crossing a salt lake – hardened only on the surface. His eyes were narrowed as if not only watching where and how he drove, but thinking about something he and Mrs Richie possibly knew. But not Mardie.

'No-o,' he said, this time drawling in his normal way when going about business or talking to strangers. 'No bets with you, Mrs Richie. I have a hunch you're likely to win. And know it.'

'You two are prattling in conundrums,' Mardie said reproachfully. 'Please talk about the scenery instead, then I'll be able to join in.'

Jard glanced down at her again. His smile was in his eyes only. But it was a good smile.

'Look over there . . . as far as you can Across the right bumper,' he said. 'You'll see the Dig-in coming up now. That will be scenery enough for you for one day, Mardie. Satisfied?'

The Dig-in was a wide brown flatland of a place. Spinifex and low-growing tired-out ground-bushes broke the worn, barren pattern of the area as far as the eye could see.

A line of rectangular bunk houses stood part-sheltered on the south side of a long hump of hill mounds. The mess-hut could be distinguished from the others only because it stood a little apart, was bigger, and sported a chimney with smoke coming from it. The First Aid hut – one of Joanna's provinces – bore a large Red Cross insignia.

Near, and in the far distance, stood two drilling rigs. Mardie had seen them from the air. They were tall, steel-legged tower things. Near the top of each was a kind of platform where men – the Roughnecks – steel-hatted for protection, stood. On the near one Mardie could see something from somewhere deep in the earth being drawn up. The noise of it was ear-clattering.

'That's only a specimen being drawn up for the benefit of the Directors, so they can see how it's done,' Jard explained as he ground the ute to a stop in the shade of the nearest bunk house. 'They're double checking everything these days. That's since a couple of Companies a month or two back gave their shareholders incorrect information. Result – law suits and the Stock Market teetering.'

'Am I allowed to ask if they are really finding something?' Mardie said. 'Don't tell me if it's confidential, Jard. Then I won't go dropping any clangers around in the wrong place, will I?'

'You're allowed to ask and the Company has already reported that the percussion drilling – which is what they're doing now – has resulted in something sufficiently interesting sulphides-wise to justify a programme for diamond drilling.'

'Diamond?' Mardie was puzzled. She was thinking of bracelets, rings and beautiful brooches.

Jard smiled in his most sardonic way. 'Diamond is the hardest cutter of all, Mardie. The diamond in the tri-cone bit of a drill would cut through the hardest rock on earth. The percussion drill works off compressed air and only tests the possible depths of the stuff you find in the surface areas. If the results are promising they change over to diamond drilling and go for depth.'

'Hence the Directors having a "Meeting-on-Location".'

'Hence the Directors, etcetera, etcetera.'

Mrs Richie suddenly came to life again.

'What's that man doing . . . sitting on the mound over there?' she demanded. 'He's using binoculars. What's he looking for? And there's another one on the other side with a telescope. What are they looking for? Nickel up in the sky or something?'

'Nope.' Jard was thrusting his long legs out of the drive door, not even looking at Mrs Richie. 'The binocular fellow is looking for bush spies and the telescope fellow is watching to see if any low-flying aeroplane or helicopter not belonging to the Company is trying a come-over to see how we're going.'

'Whatever for?' Mardie asked, slipping out of the ute after Jard. 'The sky's free, isn't it?'

'Because they wouldn't be flying over for the sake of a free jaunt in a free sky. That's why.' Jard was wearing a half-grin now. 'The word is already about that the Directors are up here. They've got the spies wondering what we're up to. Changing from percussion drilling to diamond drilling is big news for the punters in mining markets. Our chap with the binoculars is on guard for the same reason. He's watching for spies at bush level. Like . . .' He broke off.

'Like the two men with rifles who came to the crash scene?' Mardie asked quietly. 'And who later came to The Breakaway?'

'Exactly.'

Mrs Richie had hefted herself from the ute before Jard managed to get round and open the door for her.

'I'm going over to look at the mess-house,' she said flatly. 'I'm more interested in bush cooking than diamond drilling. Whatever you two might find to talk about, I just dunno. Nickel looks like nothing more than a dull piece of grey stone as far as I'm concerned. I'd rather go see someone who can make better kangaroo-tail soup than I can!'

Mardie and Jard watched her stumpy but determined figure march off in the direction of the mess-house.

'She *is* rather a pet,' Mardie said at length.

'She wanted to leave us alone,' Jard said. 'She thinks we may have something to talk about that concerns us both.' His voice was steady, his eyes searching Mardie's.

'If she thinks it's something to do with thanking me for that stint of amateur bush-nursing I tried my hand at after the crash – ' Mardie began, feeling there was no escape from these issues now – 'then please forget it, Jard. Could we make a deal? Let's never mention that beastly crash again. You know something? It seems such an age ago – I'm just plain bored with the subject. Can't we go over and look at the camp site now? I'm dying to see . . .'

'Everything that you can see, in half an hour's time,'

Jard finished for her. 'And about the crash. Sorry, but I can't forget it. Why should I? My life was at stake. You, too, could have been killed when that bird hit. Why should I forget it?'

Mardie half leaned, half sat on the ute's bonnet.

'I give in,' she said at last. Her eyes looked anywhere except at Jard. They took in the vast distances – the brown, brown land. The loneliness of it. The incredible age of it. The wonder of it. But she would not look at him.

'When you came to The Breakaway with Mister Falldown,' she said. 'The day Joanna was there – you came to say something special. I felt it in my bones and I tried to ward it off. Please say it now, Jard. Then it will be over once and for ever. Finish. *Then* maybe we can try to forget it.'

'You go first, Mardie. I feel you have something special you want to say too. Over to you.'

'You want to know *did I have my clothes off* under that blanket, while you were unconscious? The answer is – *Yes, I did.* Your shirt off too. It was the only way to keep us *both* warm. Warm flesh gives out a heat of its own, doesn't it? We had to salvage every bit of warmth just as you have to salvage every pint of underground water you find in order to run a mine at the Dig-in and . . .'

'And make the mine a living thing. A workable enterprise,' he took the theme out of her hands. 'It was the same with that night. You had to find and salvage warmth to keep and salvage life. Water to salvage nickel – if you want it your way. I think I knew all along. It didn't take those two men and their bush antics to tell me – or all the world, for that matter. In any case, Mister Falldown told me.'

He was half leaning, half sitting on the ute's bonnet beside Mardie now, his legs stretched out before him and his arms folded.

Mardie looked not at him but at those long legs. They made something in her ache. They were so much part of him.

'Of course!' she said, her voice straining at the effort for a common-sense sound. 'Why didn't I think of it? Of course Mister Falldown would tell you! You would want to know all that had happened, naturally. And you asked him.'

'Like you said, Mardie. Of course! And because he would know the truth and he would know why. He would have known what *he* would have done . . . being a bushman. He knew what you had done, and that it was *right*.'

Mardie's eyes pleaded with him. 'Then need we talk about it any more?'

'Yes. Because one other thing happened that Mister Falldown did not know. Neither did our two rifle-carrying runaways know.'

Mardie looked at him startled. 'What was that?' She was more surprised than curious.

'There was one moment when I came-to. I saw someone . . . looking down at me. A face full of care. It was wondering, hoping, and very beautiful.'

Mardie closed her eyes. That moment when he had all but come-to! Ah, but Jard had a thing about faces, hadn't he? He had said he had once been in love because of a face. Everyone had their obsessions. Hers was fear of loneliness.

So he had seen her face – looked right at her. Then closed his eyes again. The 'very beautiful' bit was his imagination, part of the dream world that is probably part of semi-consciousness. Now he was being nice and 'chivalrous' about it because of the kind of person he was. Maybe it had something to do with relief that he was alive, not dead. That kind of relief would make anyone think *anything* they looked at was 'beautiful' – even a leafless, shadeless tree out in a spinifex desert.

'I've been a "loner" all my life, Mardie,' he was saying. 'That's because of my job. First the long months of walk-over survey to study the geology of an area and locate target points for testing. Next I follow up with my "little box" doing the resistivity survey. Seismic refraction and reflection, etcetera, etcetera. They're all "loner" jobs in proving and evaluating an underground water supply.' He paused, then went on. 'But that face – that one face – did something to me. It turned my heart over – and till then, I didn't even know I had a heart.'

'What did you think you had?'

'Just a thumping engine that kept the blood stream trickling along.' He smiled now. 'Something like the pump engine that keeps the water flowing when we're actually drilling.'

'But a face doesn't do any of those useful life-giving or mine-making things.' She was trying to talk his language his way. Or the way Joanna might have talked it. Did all scientists read everything in a scientific light?

'Mardie,' he said, looking down at her, his face serious again now. 'Don't try to make me change the subject. My heart did turn over. The real heart. It was as if an angel was leaning over me and I had been given back life. It was a pale, misty, luminous, beautiful face *because it cared.* I wasn't a loner any more. Even the memory might have been good enough, but it wasn't. I've wanted something more . . .'

He wasn't looking at her now. He too was gazing out at the brown land and the spaces and the vastness and the sort-of abiding terror, loneliness and wonder of this dry, brown, oldest land on earth.

His mood seemed to change. He stopped being a dealer in wonders. His two long legs stretched out before him, were strong and physical and firmly planted on the hard ground.

'I've wanted the promise that was in that face. I've thought about it night and day ever since. The reality of it. Could you . . .? Mardie, *will you marry me*?'

He still didn't look at her. Nor she at him. They leaned side by side against the ute and looked only at the infinite sameness, yet subtle and secret varieties of the measureless red-brown land.

She wanted to say 'Yes'. She wanted to cry it out. But she couldn't because Mr Lawson had told her he was coming to ask her this very question – but only to restore her good name. Of course he would do it in a chivalrous way. He was that kind of man. Five minutes ago she had given up the battle of trying to stop him going in for this old-world stash at knightliness. Now he was doing it magically, romantically . . . all so that *she wouldn't think* it was just a case of 'being honourable and doing the right thing.'

Her eyes filled with tears.

'I would like to believe you,' she said. 'But I can't, Jard. There's too much in it of *other people*. Other people's words. Their insinuations. At best their anticipations. You know what I mean, don't you?'

'Fine five-syllable words. You left out the only important one. It has a single syllable. What about love?'

'Ah yes, Love! You can't love a *face*, Jard, except for a very little while. One becomes accustomed to a face. And accustomed to a person. Accustomed to their ways. That's out of a song, isn't it? One should never become accustomed to *love.* But thank you all the same. What you've just said, and how you've said it, is the nicest thing that has ever happened to me. I'll never forget it.'

He suddenly stood up straight, took her hand and drew

her upright. They were standing face to face.

'And I'm damned if I'm going to let you forget it,' he said. He pulled her roughly into his arms, and kissed her.

It was a long kiss, full of ardour. Something more, too. Tenderness, possessiveness and what could be . . . could it? A kind of loving? *Real* loving?

He released her. looked straight in her eyes for an ageless moment, and took her hand again. His eyes said 'I love you! And to hell with whatever you imagine'. But she didn't believe his eyes. She couldn't.

'Come,' he said. 'Let's go and give the Dig-in a good and proper look-over. We'll tell the others later . . . when the party's on. That is, when and if you can bring yourself to say that one word – *Yes*. You'll tell me when, won't you?'

He did not wait for an answer, but she went with him – easily. Not so unhappy as she had been before.

They looked over the bunk houses and Jard told her interesting things about them. How they were built down south and brought up on jinkers. He took her over to the nearest rig where the men were just drawing up a scoop of cuttings. He showed her the core tray where the samples from the one distant trial diamond drill were laid in troughs side by side. Strangely coloured and zig-zag patterned things they were. Like giant stone worms. He showed her the map where other percussion drilling rigs were still at work. Some of them were out of sight.

The ground was here and there trenched – costeans, he called them. These were exploratory trenches dug to see whether percussion drilling was worth a try. If the precious metal was still showing recurrence and density then later they would replace the percussion drills with diamond ones.

'David's reports show a number of areas in a good strike-line where the depth of specimens promises even greater depth,' he said. 'That's what has brought the Directors up. Diamond drilling is a costly business. They need to know, and see for themselves – as Company witnesses – that the stuff is here and worth penetration with the big drills.'

All the time he held her hand, as if taking her, a child, from one merry-go-round to another.

The men on the drills, white-helmeted for protection, watched them. When Jard spoke to them they pushed their helmets to the back of their heads and grinned cheerfully. Mardie could see they liked him.

'By golly, Jard,' one of them, a foreman, said. 'You'd better show us you can bring enough water down from that lake of yours under the mesa range. We're going to need it. There'll be a mine in this or I'll eat my cone-bit.'

Jard's smile was slow but good. 'I have the water,' he said. 'You find the right stuff and we're in it together.'

'Yeah. I heard the Directors have been over your maps and reports with a toothcomb. Say, mate! How come you can get a lake the size of New Guinea underground when on top out here it's nothing but ruddy desert?'

'Ask Mister Falldown next time he comes round. He'll tell you those fellas knew all about it "all alonga Dreamtime Land." '

'Isn't the old chap coming in for the film show tonight?'

'He'll come. But like his usual hermit self, he'll sit out there in the bush and look at it from afar. You know him, Harry. He likes his own company best.'

'Yeah. You and his menagerie too. Say, Jard, how come the old fella's taken such a fancy to you? You got something special?'

Jard grinned. 'Yes. Intelligence and bush manners. You'd be surprised how the combination works . . . if you and the other chaps would just try it.'

'I'll tell 'em,' Harry said laconically. And went back to work.

SIXTEEN

Sundown came and with it the barbecue. Station people – owners, wives, managers, stockmen, roustabouts and stray visitors – all came. Some of them from a hundred to two hundred miles away. The Dig-in's cook excelled himself but many of the close-in station people brought their own contributions. The Company had had cases of fruit and salads, drinks of every variety sent up by air. From the back of Jard's ute Mrs Richie produced six of the biggest pavlovas on record. She had hidden them in two ice boxes unbeknown to Mardie. Secrets as well as marvellous cooking were two facets of Mrs Richie's warm-heartedness. The Mansells were loaded down with a great supply of the largest beefsteaks Mardie had ever seen.

The men on the rigs had stopped off an hour early and had now erected the wide screen out on the best patch between the spinifex grass they could find. Everyone had brought rugs or cushions.

There was an atmosphere of great fun and excitement. Lonely people working in lonely places knew how to make a party a wow when one was really turned on.

Jard had made introductions all round and Mardie found herself in the delightful situation of being actually and warmly 'wooed' by the Dig-in's Directors. They thought she was a 'wonder girl' to have thought up those motel units for accommodation at The Breakaway.

'Now we can come and go without having to dig down out here in the spinifex,' the Chairman told her. 'Besides, if there is a mine out of this exploration exercise – and we think there will be – we'll need all that accommodation and more. The Company's willing to finance you to double, even treble it. How's that for a bargain?'

Mardie was bewildered. 'It would take a lot of managing,' she said thoughtfully.

'Mr Lawson says hand that side of it over to the Richies. They'll manage anything, even a moon walk if the Americans want it.'

Mardie laughed. It was true. The Richies were born managers; good-willed and happy about it too.

'Why did Mr Lawson have to take off so soon?' she asked, troubled. She badly wanted to see him – mostly about what had taken place between herself and Jard.

'He had a court case due in Perth in a few days' time. He did take time to be the *first* to sign in for accommodation in one of those new units of yours, Miss Forrester. "Making history", he called it.'

'Yes . . .' she said slowly. 'He did want to do that. He, too, has a vested interest. He is my trustee. You know that?'

'Yes. He's also a member of the Historical Society, hence his interest in "making history". The best friend you ever had, thrown in for good measure.'

'Thank you for saying that last bit. I knew that myself. Before Mr Lawson took me over I was so – well – *all alone,* specially where The Breakaway legacy was concerned. It, too, is part of the history of the outback. My godfather would not have wanted it to disappear.'

'But you're not alone now?'

'No. Thanks to Mr Lawson and you all at the Dig-in, David, Joanna, and . . .'

'You haven't heard? What's gone wrong with the bush

telegraph? Oh dear! Now you're going to have a disappointment. David's accepted a transfer to our next exploration area up in the Kimberleys. He'll probably tell you about it when he can get through organizing the stoke-up for the barbecue. Needless to say, Miss Seddon will go with him . . .'

'*Joanna*? With David?' Mardie had a slightly stunned feeling. 'I thought she was wedded to the Dig-in.'

'Miss Seddon is wedded to any job she's on. She's a hundred per cent efficient, which means that any job she's on she owns. But we have good replacements we're sending up. Her work here has been excellent, and her extra services such as the First Aid Unit and as occasional stand-in for the cook, have been a boon. She'll move on and possess the next exploration field and be a boon to that, too.' The Chairman broke into a kindly laugh. 'Just between you and me, Miss Forrester, the Board of Directors sometimes think our Miss Seddon possesses the entire Company – Chairman and all.' His smile was amused but kindly. 'Not that we'd have it otherwise. A very valuable asset indeed is our Miss Joanna.'

'And she'll go? I mean she'll *want* to go?'

'She has already said so. She all but looked David in the eye and said, "Lead on, MacDuff". Give her a challenge, tough as you like, and she'll rise to it. A bit like one of those pavlovas your Mrs Richie brought over from The Breakaway. Have you had some? If not, rush it now. It'll all be gone within five minutes of the men spotting it.'

'Yes . . . of course . . .' Mardie was feeling dazier and dazier every minute. 'But Jard? I thought Joanna worked with Jard . . . some of the time. Is he going, too?'

'No. Not Jard. He's mapped water all right, but that's one thing they won't need up in the new exploration area. When the Ord River is in flood it's almost enough to keep the Indian Ocean going. Jard now has the long job of bringing the water down to wherever we put the mine. He will oversee the construction of suitable bores, the drilling and construction of a well-field. Not to mention overseeing all pumping equipment, testing of water flow and so on. I'm afraid Jard Hunter will be with the field for many a long day.'

'So Jard stays.'

There was a twinkle in the Chairman's eye as he looked at her.

'Jard stays . . . God and Jard willing,' he said. 'Ah, here comes David. Ask him how it's done, Miss Forrester. I'm only a business man. He's the professional. Now, excuse me, I'll leave you while I tackle my share of that pavlova.'

David's grin was heart-warming. 'So you've heard the news, Mardie love! I can see it in your wan smile. We're shortly to part and we're both stuck with broken hearts.'

'David darling. I've a dreadful confession to make.'

His eyebrows did a half-moon waltz. 'Don't tell me you love me all that much?' he said, teasing.

'Yes, I love you. Of course I do. All the girls do. But I'm not *in love*. Does that make a difference?'

'Not a bit if you're *in love* elsewhere. I'm always in love all over the place. But there's someone round here all geared up that way about you, Mardie. Don't treat him rough, will you? He's too good for that.'

'David . . . you're trying to tell me about Jard, aren't you? I'm so tired of playing with words I'd rather we all came out with everything we mean. I've been doing that – I mean *playing with words*. And now I'm all guilty . . .'

'Here, come sit on this fat boulder and tell Uncle Charlie all about it. He's a good listener.'

'You mean David disguised as Uncle Charlie is a good listener. Well . . . whichever you are I'm about to tell the truth. Sort-of cleanse my soul. Listening? I set you up, David. Yes, I did. I let someone think I was all that crazy about you – in the *in love* sense – he probably went away to wait for you to announce the marriage banns. That rather put you in a nasty spot, didn't it? So I'm saying I'm sorry and please forgive.'

'And Jard was the one to whom you told that heart-rending story?'

'Not told. Suggested is a better word.'

'Well, you'd just better heave yourself off this nice fat boulder and go do some *un*suggesting. That was a right cruel thing you did to Jard. You aren't that bitchy by nature, are you, darling? You're a proper little humbug.'

'Cruel to Jard?' Mardie thought David was temporarily a little mad. How could anyone be cruel to Jard? He was the hit-back kind, wasn't he?

'Yes. I'll tell you something about Jard, sweetheart. And you'd better listen hard. Jard's the most honest chap who ever lived, and I'll blast anyone off the top of the mesa who says not. But he's a loner. You know . . . the man who walks and thinks by himself. Too far outback with his work to fall in love. But at all times lonely all the same. Then he sees a girl, and click go the shears. The armour plate falls off. He's got something for her. From the boots up.'

'Who? Am I allowed to know?'

'Don't play dumb all the time, love. A girl called Mardie Forrester. Ever heard of her?'

'David. You've been listening to that beastly gossip. You, too, think Jard should jump on a white charger and gallop off to save the fair lady's name from perdition.'

'I don't think any such damn' stupid Victorian rot. What I think is this – and you listen carefully, sweetie. I've known Jard since back in University days. And I know him well enough to know he wouldn't ask any girl west of the border or south of the Timor Sea to take a ride with him on a tandem, let alone in a helicopter, unless he had a something for that girl. And a something he meant. Are you listening?'

Mardie nodded. 'Yes,' she said in a very muted whisper.

'Okay then. When they told me over the two-way from the Vet's call at Mansell's Corner that Jard had actually invited a young lady to take a joy ride with him in the 'copter, I said, Great! He's like the rest of mankind. He's fallen for a girl at last! And one thing more. I could have given a whoopee it was Mardie Forrester, the nicest pet this side of the Gibson Desert. Still listening?'

'Yes.'

'Don't turn him down, Mardie – just because there happened to be a crash and a couple of baddies looking on. Then some talking all-about. He's all for you. And he means it. He's a loner . . . always has been . . . but he doesn't want to be a loner any more. The time comes for every man when he needs a girl's companionship and, if possible, love. You got the message?'

Mardie was silent. She twisted her hands in her lap while trying to believe David's words. Wanting to believe them. Yet afraid.

'But how do you know all this, David?' she said at length. '*You* haven't a girl . . . unless it's Joanna.'

He threw back his head and laughed.

'Joanna be blowed!' he said. 'Joanna is dedicated to possessing something or someone *for the time being.* It never lasts. The Directors have put it to her to join the team on this new exploration trip up to the Kimberleys. What does she do? Drops everyone and everything else that's ever been in her mind with a clang you could hear on Thursday Island. Or as far as the black stump the other side of the Nullabor.

She's got something new to boss, bully, organize and possess. A brand new Exploration Camp. All hers. At least, that's what I'll let her think to keep her happy and at high-water mark efficiency-wise. Have you registered all that, Mardie sweetheart?'

'Yes, I think I have. And do you know, David . . . I think you're right. Joanna is a born boss, and because she is a female she has to prove it harder than any man has to prove it. So she bosses harder – seemingly.'

'Right again. And one thing more, love. That bit about me not having a girl. Come the day I have the chance I'll show you my address book. Then we won't talk about "*a* girl". It'll be "girls". Dozens of 'em.'

Jard was coming across the open space between where they sat on the boulder and the burning coals under the barbecued steaks. He was licking the fingers of one hand, boy-like.

'Must you two stay talking the whole night through?' he asked mildly. Yet under that mildness there was a question mark. Something that had a streak of determination in it.

'Well, Mardie kinda likes looking at the after-sundown sky,' David said cheerfully, getting up and stretching himself as if he, as a person, held no such interests. 'Swap you places, Jard,' he said. 'That is, if this here bush-rose will excuse me. I, too, would like a barbecued steak, a stiff drink, and some of that famous pavlova.'

He moved away, then glanced back.

'Don't forget to bring Mardie back before all the food is gone, Jard,' he said. 'Meantime I'll give you a tip. Make her face the truth . . . for a change. About who she's fallen for – love-wise. And who she hasn't. You just might let her in on *who's fallen for her,* hey? *Au'voir,* the pair of you. Good talking!'

Mardie might have blushed except that she knew this was no more than another case of David making funnies. Jard would know that too, she thought. It was all a joke. Self-made this time. So meant to be taken in fun. The only thing she could do was smile it off, the way one always did when the name of the game was *teasing.*

Jard's eyes were looking into hers. What did he think of what he saw? It couldn't be much. The day was dying and all that was left of it was the red flag of a sun already set. Not enough light in which to read eyes. He wouldn't see her valiant attempt to keep up with David's teasing, would he? She wondered what his eyes would look like if he did fall in love. What she'd dreamed she'd read in them earlier? From what the last of the sunset could tell her they reasoned with her gently. They were no longer aloof nor superior as she had first known them.

He seemed so high up, standing there. But then, he had always seemed high up, and alone in that high-upness. That was because there was no one else like him.

They were silent as if they might have so much to say neither could say anything. Mardie did not dare look quite at him.

She thought of herself as a rather ordinary *town* girl who had come up here in the wild lands of vast spaces to live. And she'd met a man with the kind of eyes that could stare straight into the sun, or measure the terrible distances of this outback with a glance.

He said nothing. But he held out his hand.

Mardie's will had suddenly gone like the wildflowers that went with the coming of the Dry and the terrible heat. It was lost somewhere in the sand dunes and over the spinifex plains.

So she put her hand in his.

He drew her up so they stood together, still looking at one another.

'Give me your other hand, Mardie.'

She did so. He held both her hands now in his two hands.

'Will you listen to me if I tell you something?'

She nodded.

'I know what happened on the night of that crash, Mardie. A little of it. Not all. That night *every now and again* I nearly came to. Not quite, but nearly. And someone was holding me, and was caring for me – with a kind of loving. I thought it was no more than the loving of one human being who was trying to help another survive. I've learnt in my life in the outback that, when you look after someone, then it is a caring that is a loving. That's what caring for is. I felt it and I wanted it to go on for ever.'

His arms had gone round her, and hers around him. Her head was suddenly on his shoulder, her face cradled in the curve of his neck. But she could *say* nothing.

'When I really came-to in that half-light,' he went on, 'someone was leaning over me and I saw her face. That is what I meant when I told you that once I fell in love with a face.'

'What was it like . . . that face? Tell me again.'

'Kind and tender. Eyes that were soft. Afraid, yet holding courage.' He paused as he rested his cheek on her head. 'And loving. That was what mattered. The blasted dizziness came over me again and I had to close my eyes. Then I wasn't anywhere. I was on my own. Hell! It was a ghastly feeling.'

He suddenly straightened up, took her by the shoulders and held her away from him.

'Not any more, Mardie. You will marry me, won't you?'

'Are you sure it is not because of those two men, Jard? And what they said? The baddies? Why were they scared of you enough to go off and not help us?'

He laughed. It was an amused laugh and held no animus in it.

'I'd caught them some months ago shifting pegs on a claim. I stood over them and made them put every peg back in its right place . . . one by one. Miles of them. It took all day.'

'Weren't you afraid?'

'No. I was the one who had a rifle that time. I've never used it except to shoot game, of course. And it's registered. But that couple wouldn't know that. They wouldn't know what I was capable of doing – *or not doing*. So they didn't take a chance, and did what they were told. Replaced the pegs. And smartly too.'

'Were they valuable claims?'

'Not for minerals. No. But for water, yes. They were The Breakaway's claims, Mardie, and even if they'd re-pegged and applied to the Warden's Court for a mineral claim they'd have won nothing. They didn't know the only treasure under that ground was *water*. And water under the ground belongs to the State of Western Australia. Not to any one, two, or a dozen people. They may use it, but they can't buy it or sell it or form a company to control it. Not even you, Mardie. Your Breakaway sits on it and can use it – give it away in gallon drums – till Kingdom Come. But you can't sell it. That's the law.'

Mardie's arms tightened round him. He could not see the smile in her eyes so he did not know she could now tell Mr Lawson that Jard would not be embarrassed about seeming to marry her for her mineral claims. There weren't any minerals. She must be the only person in the mining world who was, this minute, thanking God there were no such things as minerals under her claims.

'You did say something a minute ago, Jard,' she said, lifting her head and looking up at him. His face was a pale oval in the coming darkness of night.

'What was that?' He looked down at her, his eyes gentle and kind.

'You asked me to marry you.'

'Have you an answer ready?'

'Yes. It's yes. And, Jard, I do love you very much. Since the day you first walked across the bitumen on to The Breakaway's gravel, I think. Even if you didn't ever come to love me . . . or even like me, you were someone for me to wonder and think about. It was as if I had someone in *my* heart to keep me company.'

'Now we both have company.'

'For ever.'

'And ever. How about our going to tell Mister Falldown? He's out there in the bush somewhere. He'll be able to promise us that after this life we'll still have each other in his Dreamtime World.'

He bent his head and kissed her. It had caring-for as well as love in it. Then something warmer, and possessive – but in a wonderful way.

'*Mine!*' he said, and meant it.

Night had fallen and the blue-black skies were pricked with stars.

It was by the faint light of these stars that Mrs Richie, coming towards them laden with two beefsteaks and two wedges of her pavlova cake, saw them.

She stopped. With her head on one side she stood and looked.

'There you are!' she muttered to no one in particular, unless it was to the night owl, sitting silent and watchful on the branch of an ancient bush scrub. 'I said there'd be a party at The Breakaway inside a month. I must tell Mr Richie to order some special stores. And not another day lost. Dearie me . . . who knows but the next thing will be a new house on Mansell's Corner.'

Then she was struck by another more brilliant thought. 'Grandchildren for me and Mr Richie! You never can tell what will happen next in the outback, can you?'

The wise old owl on the tree branch had an answer to that – but he did not make it known.